VIA Folios 155

The Sons of the Santorelli

Cover design by Karen Bright.

Library of Congress Cataloging-in-Publication Data

Names: Taddei, Tony, author.
Title: The Sons of the Santorelli : stories / Tony Taddei.
Description: New York, NY : Bordighera Press, [2022] | Series: Via folios ; 155 |
    Summary: "In an unsentimental departure from the conventional immigrant
    family saga, the linked stories of "The Sons of the Santorelli" feature the collision
    of great hope and whittling circumstance. Tony Taddei invites us into the
    home of the Santorelli family with its plastic Pieta, lace doilies, and behemoth
    TV, and paints a vivid portrait of a time and place"-- Provided by publisher.
Identifiers: LCCN 2021055598 | ISBN 9781599541754 (paperback)
Subjects: LCGFT: Short stories.
Classification: LCC PS3620.A287 S66 2022 | DDC 813/.6--dc23/eng/20211123
LC record available at https://lccn.loc.gov/2021055598

Printed with Ingram Lightning Source.

Published by
BORDIGHERA PRESS
John D. Calandra Italian American Institute
25 W. 43rd Street, 17th Floor
New York, NY 10036

VIA Folios 155
ISBN 978-1-59954-175-4

The Sons of
the Santorelli

STORIES

Tony Taddei

BORDIGHERA PRESS

TABLE OF CONTENTS

THE GREAT DREAM

> The great dream of my fathers
> was to be good at doing nothing.
> — Cesare Pavese

Vittorio is sitting in a forward crouch facing a woman who's come in asking for a pair of button straps with empire heels. She's paying no attention to him, and so to correct this he glides his hand along her ankle—her silk stocking rippling at his touch—and then ever so slightly caresses her instep. American women appreciate dark, handsome men with hands that are smooth and firm and not marred by hard labor.

He releases the woman's instep to spread open the shoe's strap, separating its tongue of white leather on one side from the ivory buttons on the other. He's not looking at the shoe when he does this. He's looking at her face. And just as he feels her toes make contact with the lip of the shoe, she looks at *his* face, getting ready—he thinks—to return his smile, the one he has practiced for such occasions. These maneuvers work for him as often as not to close a sale. And if they lead once in a great while to something more than a sale, well, that's fate, isn't it?

But the woman does not return Vittorio's smile. Instead, she tilts her head toward the store manager who has been standing behind Vittorio.

"Is our salesman helping you find everything you need, ma'am?" the manager says.

"That depends on what you mean by *need*." She wrinkles her nose as if a stink has risen nearby. "Have him take these away." The woman sweeps her arm out in front of her, the disgust on her face turning into something more like queasiness. "I've decided I don't want them."

"Yes, of course." The manager turns to Vittorio. "Go. Take the shoes."

"Please, signora," Vittorio says. "We both know these are not the shoes for you. Am I right?"

"Go," says the manager. "*Now.*"

He's an ugly American with big ears, this manager with his stupid vest too tight for his belly. Sure he's got his store to run, his own problems, but Vittorio never liked this Irishman even as he had to kiss his *culo* to get this job. Though what else could he do? Bread lines. Banks locking out people too dumb to keep their money hidden in their houses. And Vittorio with four sons and a wife. If he were a weaker man he would have thrown himself under a train. But he's got a Latin charisma, a melodious half-English/half-Italian speaking voice and a way with women that he can use to make a living without the usual blood and sweat that most men have to pour forth to earn their daily bread. When God gives you a talent you use it. If he's teaching his sons anything he's teaching them that. Besides, he's no gigolo. Yes, he was a wedding photographer who got a little too friendly with the brides' mothers. And yes, he was a dance instructor who brought in more than his share of the girls (until their mothers got him fired). But what business would he ever have in being a man kept by some old *strega* with money? Then again, that might be easier than having to seduce a woman into buying a pair of shoes so he can make a few pennies in commission.

"*Per favore*, Mr. Andrews . . . sir. Allow me to service this woman further."

Vittorio has picked the words carefully. He's been studying English by reading American newspapers and though it's painful to have to ask his oldest son for help on the sounds and meanings, he's proud of his growing vocabulary. Still, right now there appears to be something wrong with how he said what he said. The manager in his Buster Brown bow tie is growing red in his cheeks, and why is that *puttana* giggling?

"I said go. Now . . . immediately."

"Sure . . . For sure. I go." Vittorio makes a show of gathering the box and the shoes, tissue paper flapping. "Goodbye, ma'am." He marches to the back of the store whistling with intent, a popular tune he's heard multiple times on the radio at the barbershop.

"I'm so sorry." Vittorio hears the manager saying to the woman. "Perhaps I can show you some other styles?" But the woman isn't having it. Vittorio can hear the sound of her footsteps all the way out to the street.

In the back room, under the latticework shadows of the rolling ladders, Vittorio drops the shoes and their box into a trashcan. If the manager comes back there looking for him, he wants him to recognize his disgust. Pride demands it.

At home his wife will be starting dinner. And his sons, they'll be somewhere too. The two-year-old, on the floor of the kitchen, putting everything he sees into his mouth; the more his mother slaps him the more things he puts into his mouth. His next youngest—so sulky and sad already at eleven years old—he'll be on the stoop of their apartment building waiting like a dog for Vittorio to come home. As to his oldest, he'll be at the kitchen table doing homework, *always* at the table doing homework (proving what to whom?). While son number two will be out stealing magazines and candy bars from drug stores and running errands for crooked men. These four sons of his, all so different and not really a trace of him that he can see.

Shifting his gaze over the lip of the can where he's thrown the shoe box, he stares down at his own shoes, the English leather wingtips with quarter point toecaps that he bought by taking money out of the mouths of those four sons of his. He reaches into the trashcan and pulls out the box, replacing it on the shelf behind the ladder.

Vittorio is walking to catch his bus and it has started to snow in New Haven. The lamplights on the sidewalk are highlighting the flakes as they fly into and melt against the hot glass. It's odd how the snow in America warms and chills him at the same time. They never had much of it on the Adriatic. But then again they didn't have much of anything but sea and rocks. The donkey his father used to make a living ate better than he and his brothers did.

Vittorio doesn't really want to go home tonight. And with the way his wife treats him—without passion or affection—and the way his sons' insatiable needs overwhelm him, it only serves them right when he sometimes doesn't come home for hours after he gets off work. A man marries because he's told he must. He has children because he's told he must. What else can he do except to show his wife and children there is something left that no one can tell him he must or must not do.

He's still trying to put to rest what happened with the woman at the store. The manager didn't say another word about it, but there was something in the man's eyes when he locked up the shop for the night that is making Vittorio suspicious of what he's planning for him.

At the corner of the street, there is a fat, blond-haired man with a child. The boy is reaching up and over the man's huge belly, but the man has his coat on and his mind elsewhere. Vittorio can tell that this father does not sense the needy pressure of his son's hand. The bus arrives and the man and his son begin to move toward it. Then, a second before the man lifts his own enormous weight onto the first plank of the bus's steps, he reaches down to pick up his son, hugging him and kissing his hair, after which he sweeps himself—more gracefully than Vittorio thinks he has a right—into the bus, the little boy in his arms.

The bus driver looks at Vittorio through the open door. Finally, he jams the lever to close the door and the bus hisses and lumbers away. Why does it feel to Vittorio that the fat man on the bus has made off with one of *his* sons?

A couple of blocks away there is a side street—an alley, really, that has always reminded him of one of those alleyways in Turin that the *capos* made him march down during the war. It doesn't have the cobblestones of a Turin street, but this alley does have a brothel where for a dollar or two a girl will take off her robe and let a man lay his face on her breasts like a baby. The brothel will have its red light on tonight, and what his wife and sons do not know has never hurt them.

There are city noises all around him, but as he begins to walk in the direction of the brothel one sound breaks through—high heels on the sidewalk behind him. He slows down to let it get closer and when he turns he can see that the shoes are expensive pumps belonging to a woman who passes him by before she stops to face him.

She is not pretty, and she is not at all young. She is thin-boned and tall, maybe sixty years old, with a nose like the hooked beak of a parrot. The creases on her face are caked with makeup, and she is wearing a fur stole with actual fox heads hanging from the collar.

"Is this the way to the Jockey Club?" Vittorio can see specks of lipstick on her teeth. Yet there is something about the way the large diamonds in her bracelet are twinkling that makes him start to set aside the idea of the brothel.

"Yes, *signorina*, this is the way." He looks at her starched white gloves and the fat evening clutch she's pressing against her bosom. "If you like, I show you."

The screaming brass from the horn section of the ten-piece orchestra in the Jockey Club is starting to hurt Vittorio's ears. The woman in the fox stole insisted he come inside to meet her friends (though she didn't have to insist too hard), and now he's sitting with all of them at a round table not much larger than one of the cymbals being beaten by the drummer in the band. These two friends of the woman are as old and overly made up as she is. They're sitting so close that he can smell the sour fumes of their breath that they've tried to hide with mints.

The woman in the fox stole takes a cigarette out of her purse and poises it between her fingers. He's been lighting their cigarettes and calling waiters over since he first sat down—there's no alcohol being served openly, but the waiters have been bringing round after round of cocktail glasses filled with ginger ale and colored syrups. Vittorio taps open the box of matches that the club has placed on the table and he strikes one toward him, putting on a show of protecting the woman from the flame with his own hands until he can tame it and lift it toward her lips. She sucks in the heat and breathes out the smoke, making no attempt to keep it from streaming into Vittorio's face, grinning in a way that she must think is seductive.

"Dance with me." The woman to Vittorio's right removes the bolero jacket she's been wearing and adjusts her dress to show off her sagging décolletage.

"*I* have the first dance," says the woman Vittorio came in with. She crushes the cigarette he's lit into a brass ashtray and puts out her hand for Vittorio to take it. But the third woman, directly across from him, thrusts out her arm and puts her fingertips on her friend's wrist.

"I have a better idea," she says. She cocks her head toward the back of the club.

Following where the tilt of her head is leading across the dance floor and through the crowd, Vittorio spots a row of twelve or fifteen slightly undersized doors, curved at the top like the doors that trolls live behind in fairy tales. It's the first time he's noticed these doors—they could be the entrances to so many men's and ladies' rooms, except that there would be no reason to have that many men's and ladies' rooms in a place like this. Also, each of the doors has a Black man standing next to it at attention, all of them dressed like jockeys in half-helmets and tight white breeches that accentuate their thighs and buttocks. One of the jockeys is staring at him. What is he looking at?

Before Vittorio has a chance to ponder it further, the jockey breaks eye contact and opens the door he's guarding. From out of the room behind the door, a group of men and women come stumbling back into the club's dining salon. Their clothes are disheveled and they're laughing.

"Wicked," says the woman in the bolero jacket.

"Yes." The woman Vittorio came in with grabs her fox heads off her chair. "What in God's name are we waiting for?"

The private room is so tiny that it can barely hold the two red-leather banquettes placed one on either side of the low cocktail table. With the slightest extension of an arm or leg, anyone sitting there would be in intimate contact with the people sitting around him.

The women ask Vittorio to order a third bottle of champagne along with another bottle of bootlegged bourbon. The jockey delivers them, and the woman in the fox stole takes Vittorio's arm and pulls him down onto the banquette between her and the woman who'd been wearing the bolero jacket. Sandwiched between the two sweaty women, sitting three abreast where there is barely room for two, Vittorio begins to fidget.

They are wrinkling his trousers and crushing his shirt collar, and as he tries to smooth his pants and pinch his collar back into shape, they start to pull off his tie. At home, no one but his wife is allowed to touch his clothes, and then only to wash and iron them. Even during his dalliances with other women he is the one who maintains control of the jacket and tie and shirt. But these women seem to have no respect for him or anything, including his clothes. The woman in the stole tosses his necktie across the room, laughing at him. And when he makes a move to go over and pick it up, the women pull him back again.

What right do they have? None of them has yet made an offer to pay him. And who will be expected to foot the bill for all this liquor?

"You're so handsome." The woman in the fox stole rakes the tips of her emerald-green fingernails along Vittorio's cheeks. "So delicious. Make love to us . . . *please.*"

"What about me?" says the woman on the opposite banquette.

"I said to *us,* didn't I? Come on, let's push this table out of the way so we can all get closer."

Vittorio wants to assume that the woman in the fox stole has used the term "make love" as they do in the moving pictures: to flirt with them using his eyes—as would his hero Rudolph Valentino—speaking to them seductively. She couldn't possibly mean anything else, could she? Not here when that jockey could come shuttling back in at any time.

Vittorio pictures the jockey walking in to throw a saddle on him that the three women then take turns sitting on to ride him around the room.

"Shall we lock the door?" The woman who was wearing the bolero jacket now has more buttons undone to further expose her cleavage.

The three of them laugh and the woman who's been sitting alone goes to the door to bolt it. "Let's push these banquettes closer together," she says. "We need to get more comfortable."

"Take off my shoes, *Daddy.*" The woman in the stole raises the heel of one of her pumps to Vittorio's cheek before dropping the full weight of her foot onto his lap and mashing it into his groin. "Take it off."

He begins to unbuckle the shoe then stops and looks into the woman's eyes. She has to see that he's pleading with her to call this off, to leave him his dignity. But she only smirks, finds her handbag on the floor, fishing out a twenty-dollar bill. She hangs it in the air in front of Vittorio's face then lets it flutter into his lap. He swallows to relieve the lump in his throat, and goes back to the buckle where, with every small movement—the prying of the prong from the hole of the strap, the prong's release from under the strap, the strap pulling free—she drops another twenty into his lap. This or something like it has always been his great dream: money for doing nothing, or next to nothing. Though the thought of it now gives him little joy.

The woman runs her hand through his hair, mussing its carefully oiled part, then leans over to kiss him on the lips. Not asking, just doing it. He can't make himself look at her, so he fixes his eyes on the shoe he's left holding. The stitching is perfect.

Somewhere, a *man* made this shoe.

He's been wandering for more than an hour when he finally stops to stand in the doorway of a five-and-dime that has been closed for the night. The slush from the snow that's turned to ice water is ruining his shoes, the patina he works so hard to keep alive on the leather. With his hand in his coat pocket, he finger counts the five twenty-dollar bills the woman gave him. Twenty, forty, sixty . . . it's more money than he makes in two months of working at the store. He crushes the bills in his fist.

Across the avenue a policeman comes out of a side street, turning onto the main drag. He's wearing a double-breasted uniform coat with two rows of brass buttons that taper into a V from his collar to his crotch. He looks like he's having trouble holding up the bulk of his body but when he spots Vittorio huddled in the doorway, he stands up straighter and lifts the brim of the cap he's pulled down over his eyes. That look: in the eyes of America, he will always be a greasy Italian, a hoodlum, committing a crime by standing there and breathing the air. But Vittorio would rather not have to explain how he got the money in his pocket. So he steps from the doorway and heads uptown.

He'd gotten out of that room as quickly as he could after those women toyed with him a while longer. It never did come to sex. Not really. Though it might have been better if it had, given what he had to do for the money that was thrown at him.

Reaching the alley that reminds him of Turin, he finds the red light glowing behind silk curtains in a first-floor window. The money he got from the woman will buy him as many hours here with as many women as he can handle. Maybe the whole night happened to get him to this moment. He can almost feel God's hand reaching down to guide him.

He starts up the stoop of the building but then hears footsteps followed—before he can turn around—by a "thwack" and pain in his ankle so massive that it brings him to his knees.

"Where you think you're going, you guinea bastard?" The cop from the five-and-dime pokes his nightstick into Vittorio's face. "Get the fuck out of here you dirty wop."

Vittorio struggles to his feet. If he had any fight left in him he might argue. But after what's happened to him tonight he has a much clearer picture of his own weakness.

Three blocks away, when he's sure the cop is no longer behind him, he stops outside a park and sits on a bench. His ankle is throbbing. He closes his eyes and reaches down to feel the swelling.

Maybe he should take this money in his pocket and go to the hospital? Or maybe he should use it to buy a gun and shoot himself like the crippled animal that he is. Then again, he might take the money and limp home to his sons. Maybe he could use it to teach them something.

Though, right at this moment, he has no idea what that would be.

THE SONS OF THE SANTORELLI

Their mother is running a feather duster over the body of Jesus. None of the Santorelli boys have ever paid much attention to this small-scale porcelain replica of Michelangelo's *Pietà* and watching their mother work, they don't think much about it now. It's 1937 and this statue of Mary cradling Jesus has been on the shelf atop the scrollwork radiator cover next to the kitchen window for as long as any of them can remember. Nothing unusual, just an object their mother reveres, which also happens to be a statue of someone else's mother holding the body of her dead son.

"Cut the bread," says their mother, Aida. She's waving the feather duster toward a knife that's been stabbed at an angle into a breadboard, the handle cantilevered over a massive loaf with a layer of flour adorning its dome. Returning her attention to the statue, she works her index finger into a crevice between Jesus's ribs where they lay against Mary's breast. With her fingernail she flicks away a speck of dirt. "The bread," she says. "cut it before you father gets home."

But none of the boys move. Neither Carlo nor Angelo nor Eddy. And Gino, at two years old, he's useless to the task.

Carlo, the oldest by five years, is doing his trigonometry homework a few inches from the bread on the table. Eddy has a pair of dice he's gotten from some older boys and he's rattling them across the linoleum, hoping to roll a twelve, his age, as he attempts to climb the ladder of dots, throw-by-throw, from snake eyes to double sixes. Angelo is staring out a window, the way only an anxious ten-year-old in too-tight, hand-me-down shoes can stare. Gino is on the floor setting up and knocking down a tower of alphabet blocks: E, J, T, P, M, S, O. Great fun, stacking them and knocking them down, again and again.

On top of the radiator, Mary bears witness to Aida being ignored by her sons. Aida knows the Virgin watches, and she is ashamed. To be judged by Mary, the mother of all mothers. To be seen like this. Would it have been too much to ask? To have even one son as respectful to his mother as Jesus was to Mary? Aida can imagine herself cradling the dead body of one of her own sons. Or maybe one of them is cradling her body. If only they knew how flimsy life was, they'd cut the bread for her without having to be asked a second time.

Resting the duster beside the statue so that one of the ostrich feathers covers Mary's chest, Aida pulls the knife from the breadboard.

"I would have cut it, Ma," says Carlo without looking up from his homework.

She holds the knife steady above the bread, pointing the tip of it at her son.

"Let me cut it, Ma." Carlo gingerly takes the knife and begins to hack at the loaf.

"Ass kisser," Eddy hisses, cocking the dice, releasing them to clatter against the wall.

"I would have cut it too, Ma." Angelo turns from the window through which his father is still nowhere to be seen.

"You're an ass kisser too."

"Shut up, you." Aida glances sideways at Eddy and then she finds the knife and takes it from Carlo. "You're making a mess."

Carlo tries to reclaim the knife from his mother but she's not having it.

"Do your books."

Gino knocks down the blocks again.

Picking up from where Carlo left off, Aida saws at the bread with the knife. Flour whiffs off the top. She thinks of smoke. She thinks of the Holy Spirit. She can get dozens of slices out of a loaf this big if she cuts it right, but nobody ever notices how many slices she cuts; they keep eating until it's all gone. They'd keep eating until she was gone too and only when they were hungry again would anyone notice—these sons of the Santorelli and even the Santorelli himself.

Aida glances at Mary, the ostrich feather shielding her torso like a burlesque dancer. Such shame. Her son Jesus multiplied loaves to feed a mob, and still it was not enough to stop them from killing him. Aida understands now why Mary's head is tilted down and away from the gaze of any other human. It isn't shame or pity. It's guilt that she could never do enough to save her son. No matter that he is the Son of God; once she put him on this earth, like all children, his death was already written.

"I'm hungry, Ma," Eddy says, giving the pair of dice to his baby brother Gino who immediately puts one of them in his mouth. Eddy reaches for a slice of bread but before he can get to it his brother Carlo knocks away his hand.

"We gotta wait 'til Pop gets home."

Gino, flicking the die with his tongue, inhales it. Confused, he begins to gag. Hearing him choke, Aida drops to her knees.

"Fuck Pop." Eddy ignores the rap on his hand and takes the piece of bread. Carlo, infuriated, slaps his brother across the face.

Meanwhile, Aida has her fingers in Gino's mouth. His eyes are wide. She's hoping that the Virgin Mother on top of the radiator will intercede to help her clear her son's windpipe, not yet aware that her two oldest sons have their hands around each other's necks.

When Carlo and Eddy upend the table, Aida hears it go. But she keeps digging in Gino's throat. Whatever was on the table is now on the floor—the knife, the cutting board, the slices of bread, the books. Carlo and Eddy rumbling and kicking and scattering all of it while Aida wills her focus, prying at the die lodged between her baby's tonsils.

Eddy pins Carlo to the floor, kneeling on top of him, pressing his hands down on his brother's face, while Carlo tries to stick his fingers into Eddy's eyes. Seeing the hand coming, Eddy bites Carlo's fingers until the edge of his teeth breaks the skin halfway to the bone. Carlo yelps. Slices of bread are flattened and globs of blood fly onto the pages torn out of Carlo's notebooks as the boys unspool from the middle of the kitchen to the pantry to the window where Angelo cowers.

Aida, aware her kitchen is being destroyed behind her, jerks her hand out of Gino's mouth to thump him on the back. Thump. Thump. Thump. She lowers the heel of her hand to the space between Gino's tiny, chicken-wing shoulder blades and thumps again and again until—ready to kneel before the Virgin on the radiator and beg her to save the boy—the die pops out of Gino's mouth landing a few feet away, four pips facing up.

It's a moment's reprieve that's quickly blotted out by her older sons going at it on the floor, grunting and clawing and punching. Nevertheless, Aida decides that some direct thanks are in order for the resurrection of her baby son and ignores Carlo and Eddy for a few seconds more, rising toward the body of Jesus. She wants to kiss his feet in gratitude to both Him and his mother before she attempts to pull apart her sons and mop up the damage.

At the same time, Eddy feels Carlo go slack, but rather than immediately claim victory, he takes the opportunity to slap him one last time. This accomplished, Eddy jumps off and raises his fists in the air, backing up into the radiator where Mary and Jesus are waiting for him.

Seeing the statue wobbling and about to fall but not being close enough to stop it, Aida screams with such panic that she doesn't notice the shadow looming behind her. Her husband. Vittorio. He's emerged from out of the front room and is lunging toward the radiator where he catches the porcelain *Pietà* like an outfielder diving for a ball.

Having saved the statue, Vittorio Santorelli raises it for all to see. "It's safe," he seems to be saying. Though "safe" is not a word Aida would use to describe the scene.

Taken more by his father's heroic maneuver than by the man's sudden, timely appearance, Eddy forgets himself and beams at his father in pride. Vittorio nods his head; and, thinking all is well, Eddy laughs. Carlo, moaning on the floor, knows that all is *not* well, as does Angelo, who is holding little Gino in his arms, his back pressed up against the wall. Aida, for her part, waits for what will come next.

Vittorio lays the statue on top of the radiator without a sound. He puts two fingers to his lips, kisses them under his pencil mustache, and then places them on Mary's forehead. Crossing the kitchen to where his oldest son is draped on his side next to the overturned table, Vittorio reaches down and offers his hand. Carlo takes it and, in the quiet, Vittorio motions for Eddy to come.

With his oldest sons close enough now, he surrounds them with his arms in a way that could be read as loving in other circumstances.

Slowly then, he brings them both down to the floor until all three of them are on their knees. He positions the boys precisely so until they are facing him, and then he reaches back and picks up the bread knife that sits a few inches from the sole of his shoe as if someone has placed it there for him.

Without a single wasted movement, Vittorio raises the knife and lays its long cutting edge horizontally against the underside of Eddy's chin, the tip of it a centimeter from Carlo's Adam's apple.

"I will kill you if I find you this way again." Vittorio presses the knife more tightly against Eddy's chin, poking it into Carlo's neck until it puckers the skin. "I have put you on this earth, and I will take you off of it."

Aida makes the sign of the cross. He is boasting, her husband. Of course he is. It's merely a threat, a way to get the boys in line. She crosses herself again. And then again and again until Vittorio lowers the knife and the two boys crumple, terrified and spent.

At that, he leaves the boys on the floor to walk into his bedroom until his table can be reset and his dinner served. Aida moves quickly in his wake. This time all four of the boys begin to help her without being asked. Carlo rights the table. Eddy rights the chairs and scats around to retrieve pieces of bread. Angelo finds the torn pages of his brother's book and makes a wrinkled pile of them on the table where they originally sat. Even Gino neatly stacks his blocks, which this time he does not knock down.

On the radiator, Our Blessed Virgin Mother is smiling. No one can see it, but Aida knows she is. It doesn't take much to please the Virgin. With a dead son in her lap, she's simply happy to see that the sons in this room have finally caught on and that their parents have done their job, no matter how ignorantly they might have bumbled into it. A little death hangs over each of us, each day we are alive. And if a mother and father can't save their children from death, the least they can do is remind them of it.

SONGS FOR SWINGIN' LOVERS

The hooker had locked herself in the mop closet next to the kitchen at the back of the club. "Come on out of there, baby," said Eddy, rattling the door. "Nobody's gonna hurt you. I only want to make sure everybody gets in on the fun."

It was 1960, Eddy was flying high, and nothing was going to get in the way of this stag he planned. Everybody said that Eddy was the king of the stags, and he'd put this one together, paying extra attention to the details, because—after all—it was for his youngest brother, Gino. You only had one kid brother, and Eddy wanted to show every guy there how he treated this kid he loved the night before he got sentenced to a life of marriage. A man had to have a cause and Gino had become Eddy's.

Eddy himself carried the beer and liquor, the rum cake, and records into the hall that afternoon. He had checked on the veal Parmesan and ziti when his pal Tiny Tedesco brought them into the club kitchen from the walk-in refrigerator on Wooster Street where Tiny had taken them out of a restaurant that owed him a favor. He even hung up a few balloons and streamers and then, as a final touch, he found a guy who knew a guy who could get him a hooker.

"How many times do I have to say it?" the hooker called from inside the closet. "*Just* the kid. I told you. I'm not fucking the rest of those animals."

Eddy closed his eyes and took a deep breath. These whores and the rules they made up thinking they were in control or that they were saving themselves for something better.

"Go away," she said.

Eddy could hear her rattling through the long-handled brooms and mops. Was she looking for something to fight with?

"Listen, Toots," Eddy said through the door. "I got a pocket full of cash out here that says you do as many of them as you can handle any way you want—you set the rules—as long as you actually fuck my brother. How about that?"

There was a pause for about fifteen seconds before the hooker spoke back through the door. "How much you *got?*" she asked.

Eddy reached into the right trouser pocket of the tailored suit he had picked up that afternoon at Epstein's on Whalley Avenue. He pulled out a roll of bills—twenties and fifties he let coil out into the palm of his hand—and then he did a quick calculation. Twenty or so guys in the hall who might want some of this. What could she ask: twenty-five, thirty a guy? Let's say thirty-five a guy. He might or might not have enough cash in his hand.

He reached into the inside pocket of his suit jacket, sliding out an alligator billfold given to him by his wife, Rita, and likely bought with money taken from his own pocket. Truthfully, Eddy never liked this wallet all that much and he almost never carried it, but he had taken it along tonight, stuffing twenty or thirty extra small bills inside it for just such an emergency. He fanned out the bills he had tucked between the skins of the billfold. With the wallet in one hand and his roll of bills in the other, Eddy turned back to the door.

"I got enough, doll," he said. "As much as you need. Don't worry about that."

The skeleton key-driven deadbolt under the doorknob slid back and the door opened. Eddy smiled at the hooker. She looked back, but what she showed him was nothing close to a smile of her own. With her hand-tooled black eyebrows, pancaked crow's feet, Aqua Net-crisp hair and tobacco-yellow teeth that looked like they could bite the rim off a rocks glass, she was less like a living person and more like something you'd find in a wax museum.

"You better have enough," the hooker said. "I'm going to go into the ladies' room now to freshen up and in five minutes you can come in with the cash—fifty a head, in advance."

"Are you fucking kidding me?" said Eddy.

"No. I'm not fucking kidding you. Fifty a head, and I call the shots about what they can and can't do. If you don't like that you can all jack each other off."

"Okay . . . Okay," said Eddy.

The hooker turned her back on Eddy and thumped down the hallway at the far end of which the words "guys" and "dolls" had been stenciled onto adjacent doors. She was a big girl, bulky hips and huge breasts with a thick neck, and he could see sweat stains under the armpits of her filmy white blouse. By the time she got to the ladies' room door she was breathing heavily and had to stop for a minute before she opened it to slip inside. What was going on with this woman? She wasn't all that healthy, that was for sure, and it worried Eddy to think of what was wrong with her—drugs or disease or God knew what else. If he hadn't committed himself to this party, he might have simply paid her off and let her go home.

Eddy leaned back against the wall and took a breath. He had the roll of cash in one hand and the billfold in the other. Rerolling the bills into his pocket, he was about to holster the wallet back into his suit coat, when he saw a photograph he'd forgotten he'd placed into the wallet not long after his wife gave it to him.

He had always loved this picture taken on his confirmation day of him and his brothers Angelo and Gino as kids. In the picture, Eddy's left hand was on the small of his brother Angelo's back. It looked like he was getting ready to pick Angelo's pocket, the two of them twelve and ten years old respectively, and Angelo oblivious to all of it as usual.

Getting ready to slip the picture back into his wallet, Eddy caught sight of his brother Gino at the bottom of the frame, his two-year-old head poking above the picture's scalloped white edge. Gino had a pacifier in his mouth, and this view of his baby brother was maybe what Eddy loved most about the picture. Their mother would not take that pacifier out of Gino's mouth for another year, but when she finally did, Gino would begin talking nonstop. It was cute at first, but after a while it got annoying and that might have been where it ended if Eddy hadn't stepped in when he did to teach his brother how to talk in a way that made people listen.

Eddy was proud of the man he had turned Gino into, and the fact that kid was now a twenty-three-year-old rookie cop about to marry a girl that he'd gotten pregnant didn't change anything about that. Not one bit. Eddy loved Gino and to prove it, tonight he was going to make sure that his kid brother was the first one to get laid.

Returning to the hall after paying off the hooker, Eddy walked in on a craps game in full swing at the back of the room. With fifteen or twenty guys standing around screaming at a shooter on his knee, he'd spotted the commotion for what it was as soon as he turned the corner out of the bathroom hallway. It had gotten so loud and out of control over there at the far edge of the hall that no one had noticed the Sinatra LP skipping on the record player that Eddy had set up next to the open bar.

"Anything goes . . . anything goes . . . anything goes . . . anything goes . . ."

Eddy revered Sinatra and it was killing him to hear his beautiful vocal cords forced to hump out those same four syllables over and over again. He skidded over to the turntable and picked up the needle off the record.

"Hey," Eddy called into the craps game. He replaced the tone arm of the record player onto the little stem that disarmed it and yelled again, much louder this time. "Hey, assholes."

But no one against the back wall so much as turned their head. And then Eddy saw who was kneeling on the floor, crouching with the dice in his hand.

"Get off your fucking knees, Gino," Eddy shouted.

Gino, skinny and tall, wearing sharkskin pants and a two-tone rayon shirt, looked over his shoulder at his older brother approaching.

"You fuckers," Eddy hissed. The gamblers stared at him, heads cocked like dogs. "What're you doing getting him into a craps game while I'm gone? You trying to cheat him, you sons a bitches?"

"I'm watching out for him," said Eddy's brother Angelo. "Nobody's cheating him."

"Nobody's cheatin' me." Gino's voice broke when he said this.

"How the fuck would either of *you* know if you were getting cheated by these gorillas."

"Nobody's gonna cheat your kid brother," said a bruiser named McGurk.

McGurk was a friend of Eddy's who Eddy knew he couldn't really trust, owing to the fact that McGurk was not Italian and could never be a friend of *theirs*. Then again, who *could* Eddy trust in this gang of swindlers, Italian or non-Italian, made or not made? The only one he was sure he could trust was Gino and that was only because Gino was young and still believed that you had to respect age plus family, no questions asked. God help Eddy if Gino ever figured out otherwise, which brought Eddy back to the rest of these cheating bastards.

There wasn't a guy in that craps circle that Eddy was one hundred percent sure of. Not one of them would he completely count on to stand up for him if there was something better to be had by standing up for somebody else. Not Pete Romano and his huge gut and that stupid, piece-of-shit, pearl-handled thirty-eight he kept tucked in the ass band of his pants. Not that half-a-midget, Chilly Marcatto, with his overlarge head and that donkey cock everybody said he had, women supposedly lining up outside the backroom of the newspaper store he kept as a front. Not Mickey McGurk or Fuggy Belmondo or Hiney Hollerbach or Whitey Campbell or any of those other non-Italian guys who could never be *made* and who didn't deserve to be anyway, given that their people came from places where they ate their own horses and sold their own grandmothers and drank themselves into coffins that they then poured liquor into so they could keep drinking in hell. No. Only his baby brother Gino might Eddy be able to really trust out of the people in this crowd, and maybe only Gino if Eddy kept him close for as long as he could.

"Gino, get over here." Eddy was now ignoring McGurk and the rest of them.

"Whadda you want?" said Gino, not able to look his brother in the eye.

"Never mind what I want. Get the fuck over here."

Gino handed the dice to his brother Angelo.

"Angelo," said Eddy, "give me those fucking things and go start up the record again. The rest of you go grab a couple more drinks and sit tight."

"Hidie Ho," said Fuggy Belmondo, "Pretty Eddy's got a broad waiting for us. Don't you, Pretty Boy?"

Eddy hated this street name he'd been given. Yes, every guy had to have a handle, but why did his have to be "Pretty Boy?" He was good looking—a full head of wavy hair, blue eyes with long lashes—better looking than any of these other jerks. But he always thought this particular handle made him sound like something less than a man. He told the guys under him to stop using it, but Fuggy was drunk and drunken men did stupid things. Eddy would let it go for now and then later on find some reason to give Fuggy a beating so bad he'd wouldn't be able to *think* of the words 'pretty boy' for a good long time.

"Yeah, that's right, Fuggy," said Eddy. "I got something waiting for you."

Fuggy grinned and stumbled toward the bar and the rest of the craps game followed him. Gino tried to slink past too, but Eddy grabbed him by the back of his neck.

"What do you think you're doing playing in a dice game with these criminals?"

"I was having a good time," said Gino. "You told me this was my night and I could do anything I wanted and I wanted to play craps. I was doing good too."

"How the fuck do you know how to play craps?"

"They were teaching me. I was really getting the hang of it."

Eddy tilted his head toward the ceiling. *Madonna*, how stupid could this kid be? Hadn't he managed to teach him anything? What was he going to do when he couldn't watch out for his brother anymore? What was going to happen to baby Gino when the world got out of control and rolled over him like a train? And it would get out of control. And it would roll over him. There was no end to the bad things that could happen if you took your eyes off the world or the people you loved who lived in the world.

Eddy heard the ear-jangling pop of the phonograph needle being slung onto the lip of the record. Angelo had reset the tone arm back onto the first track of the Sinatra LP.

I've got you under my skin. I've got you deep in the heart of me . . .

"You said it was my night, right Eddy?" Gino was pleading with Eddy now. "I figured it was okay. You told me to have fun."

Eddy put his hand at the back of Gino's head, against the stiff bristles of his police-issue crew cut. Then he palmed the boy's face toward his, chin to cheek.

"Listen, sweetheart," Eddy said, "stick close to me okay?"

Gino nodded, his head keeping time to the beat under the lyrics of the song.

Use your mentality, wake up to reality . . .

"And try not to be stupid," said Eddy. "You got no idea all the things that can go wrong when you get a little bit stupid."

The party with the hooker began more or less as Eddy had planned. Despite the fact that she was sweating heavily under her makeup and looked more tired and red in the face than she had earlier, she seemed almost happy to see Eddy ushering Gino down the hall toward the ladies' room where she had set up shop. Winking at Eddy, she took Gino by his elbow, going so far as to hold the door with the tip of her stiletto so Gino could enter ahead of her. At the last minute Eddy had to coax Gino to go in there with her—some combination of embarrassment, guilt over cheating on his bride-to-be and simple fear, is how Eddy saw it. But he did finally manage to talk the kid into it and then felt a kind of pride when he eventually passed Gino over to her. It put a lump in his throat until he remembered the mob waiting behind Gino to get their hands on her.

Back in the hall now as he waited for Gino to come out, Eddy flipped to the B side of the Sinatra LP, *Songs for Swingin' Lovers*. With everyone around him chatting and drinking, Eddy searched the tracks of the record for the one song that made him feel more alive than any of the other tracks on this album. He let the needle rest on the beginning of the song, and when Angelo handed him a Scotch, Eddy nodded and smiled, closed his eyes and sipped.

It's very clear our love is here to stay . . . Eddy began to sink into a deep valley of pleasure, letting go of any doubts or worries that this evening and its planning had brought upon him. Inch by inch, he allowed himself to think more contentedly about his life. Before long he had talked himself into the certainty that he had a large cushion of very good, very rich years left to come, pushing aside that most deeply held fear of death, and bundling himself in the idea that age was not yet a threat to him and that a peaceful death decades from now could in itself be something to strive for. Avoiding a violent end by staying smart and respecting the right people—that alone was something a man could aspire to.

In time the Rockies may crumble, Gibraltar may tumble, They're only made of clay . . .

And say what you would about his guys in that room with him, they were full of life too. He might not trust all of them, but with that kind of unchained life around him how could the world ever really end for any of them, this gang who owned the town? Eddy snickered. He didn't know about the rest of them, but he had just decided that death would never get him. He was going to live forever.

He was grinning, his eyes still closed, when Gino tapped him on the shoulder. It took Eddy a second to re-place himself into the room and recollect where his brother had been and what he had been doing.

"Something's wrong, Eddy." Gino was breathing hard, nearly crying, his shirt only half-buttoned.

"What are you talking about?" said Eddy.

"I think she's dead," Gino whispered, his eyes watering. "The hooker."

"Jesus Christ." Eddy felt his contentment fading. "What'd you do to her?"

"Nothing. I swear. I didn't do nothing. We were sitting on the lid of the toilet and she was on top and then all of a sudden her eyes kind of went back in her head . . . I thought maybe she was cumming, but then she fell onto the floor and I don't think she's breathing anymore."

By then, the men in the room had seen Gino, and they had started to gather around him and Eddy.

"Everything okay with the kid?" asked Hiney.

"Yeah, yeah," Eddy said. "Kid's just having a little trouble." Hiney and the rest of them looked at Eddy suspiciously. "Stay here. All of you," said Eddy.

He grabbed Gino by the wrist and then he broke into a run, something that these guys had rarely, if ever, seen Eddy do. They all started to follow.

"Angelo," Eddy shouted over his shoulder, "keep them here. Don't let anybody leave."

But Angelo could not keep a single one of them from running behind Eddy to get a look at what was going on in the toilet.

At the door to the ladies' room, Eddy told Angelo and Gino to hold everybody back while he went inside. Stepping quickly toward the stall, Eddy began to move more deliberately. He'd spotted the hooker's legs, her high heels still on, poking out from under the opening of the door, and the sight of this spun the bathroom around and around inside his brain until he could see nothing so much as a crime scene.

At first, when he swung open the door to the stall, Eddy could only bring himself to glance at the hooker's face: her eyes open, her head resting on the base of the toilet. He made himself take stock of everything else first to buy himself some time before he let his eyes meet hers. There were her pantyhose balled up in the center of her miniskirt like an egg in a nest where she had let them both fall onto the linoleum next to her blouse and bra. There were her naked breasts hanging right and left, so large they curved around either side of her rib cage. There were her long arms and red nails. And there was her white satin purse, holding an enormous amount of Eddy's cash not more than six inches from her right hand.

Forcing himself to look at her face, for a moment Eddy thought she might still be alive. There was nothing dead about her eyes. Christ, she looked like she was smiling at him. Was she smiling at him? He reached out to put his hand on her neck. At the same moment his fingers registered that there was no pulse, the pressure that he had used to determine it nudged her head from where it was resting on the base of the toilet and it bounced onto the floor. It frightened Eddy in a way he hadn't been frightened in a good long time. He had to go all the way back to his childhood to remember that kind of unexpected fear.

"We're coming in, Eddy." It was Chilly Marcatto. The ladies' room door had opened a crack and Eddy could hear Chilly scuffling with Angelo to get inside.

"No," said Angelo. "You gotta stay out here."

"Stay the fuck out there. All of you," Eddy shouted.

The door slammed shut. He had to do something before all hell broke loose.

He could call a cop friend of his and they might get it covered up. Sure. But what if this hooker had a family? What if she had kids? What if she had a husband?

He didn't know her last name. He'd even had a hard time remembering that she called herself Ruby until this moment when he saw her dead on the floor of the stall.

Figuring he had at least a couple of very good reasons, Eddy picked up the white satin purse. Opening it, the roll of bills he'd given her sprung out and uncoiled over the side of her bag. At first the money, popping up like a snake in a can, surprised him. As soon as he got over that, he knew what he was going to do. Despite the voice in his head telling him it wasn't the right thing to do.

He took up the cash and rerolled it tightly back into his own pocket. It was more than a thousand dollars and there was a lot he could do with that kind of money. Besides, it wasn't going to do her any good now. What was he supposed to do, leave it for the cops to take?

With the cash tucked away, Eddy dug back into the purse. There was something else he'd been looking for. The other reason he had opened the bag.

The compact and lipstick and tissues didn't interest Eddy (truthfully, they made him squirm). But then scraping deeper into the crevices of the bag, Eddy found what he wanted: her driver's license and—as a bonus—a white business card with a few dots of black lettering.

The picture on the license must have been taken twenty years ago. In it she was thinner, a lot thinner and prettier, and she looked genuinely happy, almost hopeful, as if somebody might have given her a piece of good news. Catching sight of her name under the picture, Eddy paused and then he whispered the name aloud.

"Roberta Maria Blandini . . ."

His eyes darted to the business card, something she must have handed out to men in bars and clubs to drum up more trade.

Ruby Blades. Exotic Dancing.

He flipped the license over and looked at her big, loopy signature on the back, the way a school kid signs her name.

"Eddy, what's going on in there?" It was Gino whimpering outside the ladies' room.

If Eddy could have left this dead woman on the floor of the bathroom to grab his brother and run away, he would have, but for some reason he could not make himself do it. Not yet.

"I'll be right there," Eddy shouted.

Stuffing the license and business card back into the purse, Eddy shut the bag and placed it down next to the hooker's hand. He could feel her eyes looking at him, and as much as he didn't want to, he couldn't help himself from looking back.

"Eddy," Angelo called from outside.

"I'm coming, I'm coming," Eddy called back, though he had not taken his eyes off the hooker's face.

It wasn't going to be enough, it would never be enough, but without thinking more about it, Eddy grabbed her right hand and closed her fingers around what he'd just taken out of his pocket.

"Here," he said. Her stiffening fingers would not stay shut around the two fifties he'd given her, so he grabbed her hand again and this time he held it tight.

"Please," he said. "For God's sake, take it for Gino."

Her hand stayed shut then. Miraculously, she held on to the money.

THE WINTER BAR

He wants this first winter storm of 1968 to end now so his neighbors can watch him blow the snow off his property. All night it's been snowing. The black machine sits beside him in the garage with its swivel chute and chained tires, spindle oil and fresh gasoline perfuming the engine. It doesn't solve any of his bigger problems, but it does make him feel like a king. This Saturday morning, for once, Gino is a man who is in control. A guy who can simply chase away the snow and then stand there in his cleared driveway drinking good liquor from a shot glass to keep warm, pitying all the saps in the neighborhood who are watching and can't do what he has done.

The dog is standing with Gino in the garage, panting next to the Montgomery Ward snowblower. But as much as he loves the dog, the never-ending love he gets from the dog, and the fact that he even owns a dog, right now Gino loves the new snowblower more. Having gone ten rounds with his wife Frances to get it—fighting with her for days and finally winning on a technicality that they *had* to buy it out of their meager savings from his cop's salary if she didn't want him to have a heart attack in the driveway—Gino feels he's earned the right to show off his new machine.

Yes, he's the first of his neighbors to own one. But better than that: he's the first of the Santorelli brothers to have brought home this prize. And that is the best part of all, him being the baby brother. Him being the one who got the short end of the shovel when one of these northeast winter whiteouts trapped him, his brothers, and his immigrant parents inside their apartment where he was pushed to the head of the line to go outside and dig a tunnel to freedom.

Squinting, Gino can see that the surging snow is rapidly deleting the boot prints he tracked across the driveway when he walked from the house to the prefab garage. At the same time, the dog's paw prints are nowhere to be found. He is still not fully-grown, still no more than forty pounds of boxer and shepherd packed into a shorthaired hide. It makes sense that the dog's prints would be the first to go.

"Sit," Gino snaps at the dog. "Sit."

The dog runs in a circle around the snowblower. He barks.

"Douglas, sit down."

The dog leaps out of the open mouth of the garage. He takes a bite at the cascade of falling snow and then dives chest first into a drift.

"Dougy," Gino yells.

This fluffy, white mound where the dog landed does not seem to have met his expectations of security and warmth. Wriggling out of the drift, he returns to the garage, shaking off the melting flakes. He sits without being told.

"Good boy," Gino says.

Kneeling next to the snowblower, Gino sets the choke. The snow, although falling faster than before, is slowly thickening into larger and larger flakes. This is the storm's last gasp before it runs out of power. Gino stands, keeping his back bent, and pulls at the cord of the blower. It fires.

The dog backs up under the car, huffing, his raised fur bristling against the fender as he buries his body in shadows.

The sun is out before Gino is done cutting a path from his garage to the back door of his house. Gino's neighbor Ted Connolly is also out. He's studying Gino from under an aluminum awning that hangs over his patio. Ted has a shovel in the crook of his arm and he waves at Gino.

Gino waves back, cocky, taking one hand off the handle of the snowblower as if he's practiced this a thousand times. The snowblower cuts to the right, starting an unplanned path over Gino's buried lawn. Gino gets his hand back onto the handle but it's a second too late. Something clangs and then crunches alarmingly, making a racket in the screw housing of the blower. Momentarily, the throat of the machine is blocked. Then, heaving, it coughs up a fresh stream of snow, not the pristine fluff it had sucked up from the driveway, but a mix of slush and soil and dead grass infused with shards of yellow and red plastic.

Damn kids, Gino thinks. Toys everywhere. Ted Connolly everywhere too: always there, always watching, always giving Gino advice about everything. How easy it is for Gino to be suspicious of hairless, non-Italian guys like Ted. It's in Gino's first-generation blood. At times like this his heart pumps mistrust, and right now his heart is telling him that Ted Connolly doesn't deserve another damn thing from him. Not a recovery wave, or shrug, not even a sarcastic grin to indicate how it's Gino's belief that things always seem to go wrong even when you're trying to be polite to a neighbor. *You get punished for every good thing you do,* Gino can hear his father Vittorio mumbling. Gino running over one of his kid's toys because he took the time to wave at Ted is Ted's fault. Fuck Ted.

Gino pulls back the gear lever that propels the blower. After four or five attempts, he finds reverse and backs the machine off his lawn wishing he'd looked at the manual even once. With the tires on the driveway again he allows himself a single peek at Ted's house, but Ted is gone.

A shade rises in Gino's kitchen window. His wife is standing there, window sheers pinned apart with the thumb and forefinger of each hand, her face framed in synthetic lace. Frances is still sort of pretty, more so with the bridal veil of curtain around her cheeks, but she's getting a little chubby and their two kids are standing bosom high in front of her, which spoils it for Gino right away. It's not that he doesn't love his kids. He loves them enough. But once they arrived, Frances—curvy, little Franny Arnone who let him get so much farther up her skirt than any other decent girl ever did—started acting as if he, being a cop and all and having gotten her pregnant so that they had to get married, had put her behind bars. If only she knew how much *he* feels like the one who's in prison.

Frances is rapping on the window with her knuckle now, tilting her chin at the spot where Gino has mangled the toy on the lawn. Accusatory. Questioning.

"What?" Gino says, knowing full well his wife cannot hear him over the roar of the blower.

Frances points again at the vomit of snow, grass and broken toys.

"Okay . . . okay," he yells. What the hell does she want him to do about it now? *All I ever do is work, and all I ever hear about is what I did wrong.*

It's then that Gino notices the face of his five-year-old daughter. She is standing at her mother's side, pouting. It must have been her toy. But Gino's son, little Genie, slightly below his mother's collarbone, has a big smile on his face. Gino can't tell if the kid is smiling because he likes seeing his little sister in pain or because when the toy exploded out of the blower it was the most exciting thing that happened in this neighborhood for quite some time.

Gino idles the blower and sweeps the backs of his hands at the window, pushing them outward like a wizard who uses this gesture to clear away people who no longer amuse him. His wife and kids probably don't see it that way, though, and none of them move from the window.

"Go away," he shouts. "I'm busy out here."

Frances shakes her head with disdain; she is not going anywhere. They lock eyes, Frances and Gino, and when Gino is about to give up and ignore her—maybe for the rest of the day, if he can—she yanks the kids, not at all gently, away from the window. The last thing Gino sees before she pulls down the shade is the flame of a match as she lights a cigarette.

Hearing Gino shout, the dog has gotten up from where he's been lying in the sun by the garage and is now sitting next to Gino on the path that he's cleared. By now, the dog has become accustomed to the blower's growling and he seems to be waiting for Gino to tell him what to do. Gino waves his hands at the dog in the same way he waved them at his wife and kids, this time sweeping them toward the garage. The dog stands up.

At least someone is listening to me, Gino thinks. The dog trots back to the garage and resets himself, completely satisfied, in the sun's great light as Gino finishes clearing the driveway.

Ultimately, it's the liquor that brings Ted into Gino's yard.

It's taken Gino only thirty minutes to blow the snow off every thoroughfare on his property: driveway, back path, front path, along with a single slim alley across his postage-stamp patio from the dining room door to the clothesline. Through frigid weather tempered only slightly by sun and wool clothing, Gino has cleared his kingdom of the confusion that snow brings.

Gino is so proud of himself that, when he finally brings out the Scotch he feels is his due for the work he's done, he uses an old iron shovel to pile up a four foot high column of snow in order to fashion a kind of bar where he can display his bottle and glass. Sipping his first drink, he makes the top of his bar flatter and smoother by running his gloved palm over it again and again. Soon the bar is level enough for the bottle to sit on without rocking.

The dog has joined Gino and is taking bites out of Gino's bar, enjoying a good chew of the icy bits he finds. Gino is content to let him bite away. They seem to be of one mind, Gino and Douglas. So much so that when the dog stops chewing and looks at Gino with a question in his eyes, Gino answers him by finding a golf ball-size chunk of snow next to the bar and, dousing it with a half shot of Scotch, lets the dog eat it out of his hand.

Grrr, the dog drones lowly.

Gino is filling his glass again when Ted Connolly walks over, his boots crunching on the crystals of ice that are layering the shaded ground near Gino's house. Ted was only halfway through with his shoveling when he saw Gino come out with the bottle. At the top of Gino's driveway, before he comes to a full stop, Ted points to the blower cooling its engine on the snow-pocked blacktop.

"First time using it, huh?" he asks.

Gino nods.

Ted stops with three feet between them. He raises an eyebrow and lowers his chin toward the bottle on the makeshift bar.

"Chilly today, huh."

"You want one?" Gino asks.

"I wouldn't say no."

"Sure," Gino says, thinking, *keep your enemies close* and loving how Ted has all but groveled up his driveway for this drink. "Be right back," he says to Ted.

Gino turns and walks toward his house to get another glass. Before he reaches the back door he sees Ted's wife, Vicki, stepping out onto the Connolly's patio, zipping up her coat against the iced wind under the awning. Vicki is a blond with big teeth and an incongruously large chest who always looks to Gino like she has forgotten where she lives and that she has a husband living there with her. Vicki isn't exactly a bombshell, but with two Scotches in him and more on the way, Gino wouldn't mind finding out if there isn't something about Vicki that he's missing.

Gino opens the back door of his house. He decides he'll get two glasses to bring back outside.

They have been drinking for close to an hour when Ted remembers that he hasn't finished shoveling his front walk or driveway. During that time Gino got Vicki to join them at his snow-built bar and also invited over two other neighbors who were out clearing their front walks. There's Pat Berger, an Irish police sergeant who Gino sort of knows from the force where Gino has recently been promoted to detective. And standing next to Pat is Tony Caruso, a plumber and the only other full Italian in the neighborhood, though he's got about twenty-five years and fifty pounds on Gino. Gino waved these two over from their respective houses after Vicki joined them because he wants to have a party now in his own, snow-blown backyard.

It's the dog's barking that reminds Ted he needs to get moving again. Ignored by Gino for too long, the dog has strayed away from the group and is burrowing into the snow accumulated under a split-rail fence at the edge of Ted's front walk, not far from the spot where Ted gave up and put down his shovel. The dog starts to bark when his paws hit a fence post that he cannot wrest free with his digging.

"Douglas," Gino calls.

The dog forgets about what he's found and comes running.

Ted sees where the dog has been and drunkenly says, "I better finish up."

Vicki looks over from where she has been standing beside the makeshift bar, first at Gino and then at her husband. Along with the bottle of Scotch, there is now a bottle of bourbon and a bottle of blackberry brandy on the bar, placed there by Gino who went into the house to get them after Vicki and Tony and Pat arrived, sneaking this liquor out past Frances who has been doing laundry in the basement. When Vicki—who's been drinking the blackberry brandy—starts frowning at Ted, Gino, now on his fourth Scotch, interprets this as a sign that she might like Ted to finish shoveling their walk so she can spend a little non-Ted time with Gino.

But Ted hesitates when Vicki frowns at him. At first Gino thinks it's because Ted has caught on that Vicki might want to get rid of him. Then, he sees Ted eyeing the snowblower. Tony Caruso and Pat Berger also see Ted ogling the blower.

"Nice looking machine, isn't it?" says Pat to Ted.

"How many horses is that?" asks Tony Caruso of Gino.

"Eight or ten," Gino says, smiling with intent at Vicki. "It gets the job done."

If Gino felt any more superior at the moment somebody would have to put a crown on his head. The dog sees Gino puffed out and surer than he's ever seen him, and he lifts his haunches and resets his flanks at Gino's heels. Gino places his hand on the top of the dog's head and slugs back the rest of the Scotch in his glass before pouring himself another. The dog unrolls his tongue from his mouth and lets it hang.

"You should let Ted take it out for a spin to finish up his sidewalk," says Pat Berger to Gino.

And you should shut your drunken, German-Irish mouth, Gino thinks. As old, fat and dumb as he is, Gino knows that Tony Caruso, standing there watching this, would never do such a thing. No Italian guy would ever offer up another man's property. He's about to tell all of them to get the fuck out of his yard, when Vicki places her fingertips between Gino's glove and his coat, tickling the inside of his wrist. "Can I have a little bit more," she says, pointing at the bottle of blackberry brandy.

Right there and then, the rest of the morning and afternoon takes shape for Gino. He's got Vicki drunker than he is and undressed on a bed in a motel on Derby Avenue. He'll pay for the whole night, but they'll only need a couple of hours. Fuck Tony and Pat, all Gino's got to do is get rid of Ted for a few minutes so he can set it up.

"You ever use a snowblower before?" he asks Ted, feigning more authority than is appropriate since he himself had never used a snowblower before today.

"I know how," says Ted. And everyone in the driveway knows it's a lie.

"I'll keep an eye on him," slurs Pat Berger. "My brother-in-law Sammy got one last year. They aren't that hard to figure out." He steps closer to Ted and the blower but then stops and looks at the dog. The dog has been glaring at Pat, listening to his voice: the slurred, dishonest yelping of some creature trying to trap him and the man who is his God.

Ted makes his move toward the blower. Then Pat steps in again and Tony Caruso follows too.

"Okay, you guys have a ball," Gino says. "Knock yourselves out."

Vicki smiles at him. He doesn't quite know why, but then all of a sudden Gino understands that, in terms of Vicki, what he said to the other men was exactly the right thing to say. He couldn't have made a better move.

Gallant. Vicki thinks he was being gallant—gracious and gentlemanly, all the things that Ted is not. Gino isn't any of these things either, but he is not going to let Vicki catch on to that. He's going to let go of the snowblower now, set aside his resentment, and play this up all the way to the motel on Derby Avenue. "If you need more gas, there's a can in the garage," he calls to Ted, more loudly than he has to.

Ted, plastered with Scotch, has begun to wrangle the cold snowblower down the driveway toward the sidewalk in the front of their houses, Pat and Tony stumbling single file behind him. The snowblower has not yet been started and Gino can hear the gears whine in the blower's toaster-sized transmission, engaging in a way that can't be good.

The dog barks at the three men making off with his God's property. Then he barks at Gino.

"Quiet, Douglas," Gino says. The dog stops barking, flattening back his ears while narrowing his eyes.

"Plenty of gas," Ted yells back at Gino from out on the sidewalk. Holding the gas cap in his hand, he has closed one eye and is using the other to peek into the tank.

Gino ignores Ted. Not because he has stopped worrying about how Ted might misuse the snowblower, but because at the moment Ted speaks, Vicki flicks away a bead of sweat from Gino's unshaven chin. "You're perspiring," she says sweetly.

Not *sweating*, Gino thinks, *perspiring*. He would take her right here, right now if he could and lay her down on the snow covering his lawn.

Out on the sidewalk, Ted pulls the cord to start the snowblower, combusting the quiet of the neighborhood. Ted jams it into drive, straining to hold the blower steady as Tony and Pat shout instructions and the blower fishtails from curb to fence.

Gino pivots his head away from this melee to look again at Vicki, and it's then he sees that Frances has reappeared in the kitchen window, this time without the kids. Did she see Vicki touch his face? Not knowing either way, Gino decides to pretend nothing is happening as he smiles at Frances and raises his glass to her. Vicki also smiles and raises her glass to Frances who nearly tears the curtains off the rod, pulling them shut.

For his part, the dog doesn't seem to know what's going on. Bearing down on this puzzle, he sweeps his head right, left and center, from the kitchen window to Vicki to Gino, and then he runs full-out toward the men with the machine.

Out on the sidewalk, Ted has given up trying to cut a straight and regular path; he's too drunk and does not seem to care. Tony and Pat have run back up the driveway and, before Gino could stop them, they snatched the bottle of bourbon off the bar and ran with it back to the street where they are now laughing at Ted, egging him on to do a worse job than he's been doing.

A city snowplow turns onto the street and slows to watch the gradually building mayhem. Gino sees the driver in the plow staring at Pat and Ted. Pat has his coat off now and is waving it at Ted like a matador trying to enrage a bull as Ted attempts to dislodge the snowblower from between two fence posts where he's gotten it stuck. Tony notices the driver in the plow and lifts the bottle of bourbon toward him, all friendly inebriation. But in this scenario the driver defines sober. *Guy's probably been out since three a.m.* is what Gino thinks watching the driver shake his head in disgust at the three men with the blower.

Gino knows that the time has come to make his move on Vicki. He's torn, of course, but it's now or never. No matter what else he feels about what's happening to his snowblower, Gino knows that at this point he couldn't stop himself from trying to fuck Vicki if he wanted to. He looks at the kitchen window to make sure that the shade is down and the curtains are shut and then he curls his arm around Vicki's waist. Looking into her bloodshot eyes, he hears but does not see the snowplow's unnerving forward scrape of the street.

The dog too has watched the plow. And now that it's gone past he again turns his attention to Pat, Tony and Ted, slowly curling his lip and baring his teeth, a growl growing deep within his throat.

On the sidewalk, Tony approaches Ted and makes him take a swig from the bottle of bourbon while Ted continues to yank at the blower, trying to dislodge it from between the fence posts. Pat joins them and, after taking the bottle from Tony and pouring some bourbon into his own mouth, he wraps his hands around Ted's chest and proceeds to pull backwards, adding his unsteady weight to the task of freeing the blower.

The dog barks and barks again but the men pay no attention to him. So he barks one last time and getting no response on this final warning, he lunges at Pat's right arm.

Gino is about to whisper something provocative into Vicki's ear, and Vicki is about to listen when he hears the dog bark and looks over to catch him in the act of tearing at the sleeve of Pat's coat.

"Dougy," Gino screams.

"It's okay," Vicki coos. She hasn't been looking at the sidewalk to see what's going on. "They're only having fun." She purrs the word *fun*.

But *fun* has left the neighborhood and nothing but free will and the unchecked rights of liberty are left to take its place. Watching what comes next, time speeds up for Gino.

Pat, shaking the dog off the sleeve of his coat, backs up and raises the bottle of bourbon over his head. He's not really looking at anything other than the dog. If he were he'd see that he is standing on an icy patch of sidewalk.

Gino, however, sees the whole thing. He watches Pat swing at the dog. Missing the animal by a good foot or more, he slips on the sidewalk, his feet, legs, arms and hands rising into the air so that there is nothing to cushion his fall but the stud of his coccyx bone. Gino can almost hear the bone crack against the pavement through the roar of the snowblower.

"Are you fucking crazy?" Gino screams toward Pat on the sidewalk.

Hearing Gino's voice the dog backs away and begins to growl fiendishly at the man with the bottle sticking upside down in the snow beside him. The dog appears not to be sure if his God-man's anger is meant for him, and he seems to wants to say something about this, something to the effect of *I want to protect you, I want to defend you, I want to kill or be killed for you.*

It is at that precise moment, that Ted and Tony finally free the blower from the fence. The snowblower dislodges and they both swerve backwards. By then they have seen Pat on the ground, so as they start to lose their balance, they throw their weight in the opposite direction to avoid falling on both him and the dog.

The problem is that when Ted does finally fall he keeps one fist on the handle of the snowblower, causing the open mouth of the machine to pivot a hundred and eighty degrees, its spinning blades pointed directly at the dog. Pat, on the ground, sees what's happening and to get the dog out of the way he reaches for his front paw, that little knob of fur that seems like a perfect place to grab an animal. But the dog snarls at this gesture, biting Pat's hand, hard, before backing away slowly and right into the mouth of Gino's American dream.

Gino bellows and starts running down the driveway, leaving Vicki alone at his handmade winter bar, knocking over the bottles of blackberry brandy and Scotch as he kicks away from his desire for motel sex in a kingdom of his own making. All Gino wants now is for Vicki to disappear. For all of this to have been an illusion.

On his way down the driveway, Gino conjures up his family. There is his father floating at the top of the driveway, his backbone like a soldier's course of bricks, mumbling from under his Rudolph Valentino mustache, something about Gino being arrogant and bigheaded and too sure of himself. Gino ignores his father, but then runs smack into the image of his three older brothers blocking the path between him and his bleeding dog, all three of them snickering at Gino and how clear it is that he's still too much of a baby to handle these things this country gave him—a snowblower, a faithful dog and an easy woman who is not his wife.

By the time he skids to a stop on the ice and lies down next to the dog, Gino is whimpering: broken and empty and guilty as sin. Someone—Gino does not know if it was Ted or Tony—hit the kill switch on the blower, so it's only the tip of the dog's tail that is gone, not the whole dog. Gino makes himself look at the tail, the bleeding tip dripping into the snow, and he sees that it is wagging, beating: *I love you; I love you; I love you.*

Gino cradles the dog in his arms, resting his head sideways on the dog's rib cage, pleading for God to forgive him, trying to remember what it was like before he wanted everything he wants.

Around him in the street, Ted and Pat and Tony are trying to apologize to Gino; one of them will fix the snowblower, another says he will run to get his car to take the dog to the vet. Over on his front porch, Gino's almost-beautiful wife has opened the door and is trying to keep his kids from looking at the dog. Back in the driveway, the bottles from the winter bar have now drained into the snow. Vicki has run away.

But none of that matters any longer to Gino. All Gino will remember about any of this till the day he dies in the next American century, is the steadfast beating of the wounded dog's heart.

COMMEDIA DELL'ARTE

Act I

Two young men, naked from the waist up, walk past the driver's side of her daughter-in-law's Rambler. Sitting with her grandchildren in the backseat, Aida pretends to ignore the bare-chested men. Refusing to acknowledge their existence. *Shoo*, she thinks. *Go away.* But the men do not go away. Instead, they slow down a tick, smiling at Aida's daughter-in-law as they do. Confounded, Aida watches her daughter-in-law smile in return. Then she fixates on the men's faces. Are those smirks or grins or what … what is the word in English for a dirty smile? Okay. Enough. The men are working on her son's house and it is hot and they are young. Everything's more modern these days, more free. Boys are growing their hair longer than girls and girls are going bare-chested under the flimsy blouses they wear to lure boys. Aida understands. She understands that she would like to slap each of the men, arcing her hand and hooking her daughter-in-law Betty's cheek for good measure at the end of the swing.

It has already been a tough morning for Aida, preceded by a maddening night before. This old woman has barely gotten two hours' sleep and what sleep she's had occurred fitfully in a living room chair where she sat with swollen ankles waiting for her husband to arrive home finally at three a.m. Even now in his late sixties Vittorio acts like a man without responsibility to anyone but himself, as if he's got the keys to the kingdom and can come and go as he pleases, leaving her locked in and alone all night without a drip of remorse or any explanation as to where he's been. She argued with Vittorio all night and only stopped after he locked himself in the bedroom and she could hear him snoring faintly behind fifty years of paint swelling the jamb of the door. Then Betty showed up at eight a.m. with the two grandkids, blowing the horn for Aida to come out and get in the car. She wanted her to watch the kids once they got to this run-down house her son Angelo bought and which has to be repaired before they can move in. All Aida has ever tried to do is care for people and all she's gotten is grief and neglect from the men, women and children she's cared for. Though mostly, she'd say it's been the men.

"Come on." Aida starts pushing her grandson, Angie, out of the car and onto the driveway of the house. She wants him to exit so she and her granddaughter Tina can get out behind him. She spreads her fingers across the base of the boy's neck and shoves him. He is a mule. The girl is a bird and the boy is a mule. Aida thinks back on her own girlhood, little Adriatic bird that she was, and how her own wings were clipped early on so all she could do was hop around from one mule to the other, one man to the other—father, brother, husband—waiting on them, cleaning up after them, cooking their suppers on a stove fed by wood she carried up into the house on her own. All the time wishing she could grow her wings and fly away.

Tina sees her grandmother struggling with her younger brother and reaches around Aida to help her push. Aida can relate to this girl, can appreciate how a little girl like her has to practice for a long life of this sort of thing. The door pops open and Angie is sprung from the car like a jack-in-the-box, if the box were tipped on its side.

Reaching the back door of the house, the boy stops and stares expectantly at the bare-chested men. The men are talking now with another much older man who is standing thigh deep in a hole that he's dug lengthwise beside the foundation of the house—a long thin hole. *What do you call that kind of hole?* Aida muses. She looks at her grandson, and from the way his skinny shoulders are drooping and his pale face is tilting, she can tell he wants to jump into the hole. *A moat*, Aida smiles. *That's what you call it, a moat ... a small moat ... a 'moatini.'*

Aida would like to chuckle aloud at her own cleverness but she won't let herself do it. Why would she? She's thinking now of those teenage years before she was aware of the way some men's minds work. Arranged under the bower of a trellised grape vine, dressed as prettily as her mother would allow, she would laugh freely at one of her own jokes only to have the boy who came to court her think she was an idiot, or worse. Why would Aida, this late into in her sixth decade, ever want to forget that lesson of girlhood by laughing in front of these men in the yard?

"Angie, get away from there." Aida's daughter-in-law is yelling at her son. Aida doesn't much like Betty; so little and flimsy, too much lipstick. And always frantic, always thinking the worst will happen. Well, the worst *will* happen, of course it will, if men have anything to do with it, but using your big made-up mouth won't stop it.

"Can we go in the house?" Betty has approached the men. Slamming the door of the Rambler, Aida follows Betty, towing her granddaughter, listening in. "I'd like to see what they've done with the kitchen," says Betty to the digger of the hole.

I'd like to see what they've done with the kitchen, Aida mocks Betty from behind tight lips, hearing the wispy voice of one of those phony rich ladies she sees every afternoon when she watches her stories on the television. Those women on the soap operas are like a scab that she can't help picking. Aida closely observes the women on these shows because they remind her of the neighborhood women in the inner-city Italian enclave where she lives. The gossiping coven of Isabellas and Ericas and Alfonsinas who stop by Aida's apartment for coffee and eat her cookies and secretly judge her housekeeping, insulting her the minute they close her front door. Aida knows all about it and she keeps watching her stories because sometimes the women can be worse than the men.

"Can we go in?" Betty says again to the digger.

"Go in," says the man in the hole, shrugging and then using his shovel as a crutch to help him climb out of the trench. "It's your house."

The way he's said the word "house," with a sneer, as if he's not the one digging a hole outside a house. And why exactly *is* he digging that hole anyway? Aida sidesteps the man with the shovel and tilts her body over the pit in the ground.

"Careful, lady," says one of the younger men. Aida glares at him with a look that could boil water. Sure, let a six-year-old boy get close enough to fall in, but if a woman gets too close you have to stop her, huh? She can feel the power in her arms from years spent rolling out dough and wheeling manure into gardens, and she can feel herself using it to knock this sweating buffoon into the moat. Or is it Vittorio she'd like to toss into this hole, so similar in width and length to a grave? She quickly exorcises this thought with the sign of the cross.

"What's the matter?" Aida's daughter-in-law is speaking again to her son. The boy is squirming and tensing, clenching and then wiggling, his hands hovering at his backside, trying not to grab at the cheeks of his buttocks.

Aida already knows what is the matter.

Act II

"I have to go," says the boy to his mother.

"Where you have to go?" Aida says, butting in before his mother can pamper him like a prince. Staring at her grandson, she waits for him to answer her until finally he moans, "I have to go to the bathroom."

"Jesus," Betty says before Aida can say another word. "Can't you hold it a few minutes?"

The boy shakes his head *no*. "I gotta go number two," he says.

Aida hears Tina starting to giggle. She doesn't have to look at the girl hiding behind her big head of dark curls to know how giddy this is making her. Aida understands the girl. She *was* this girl. This girl is somewhere inside Aida still.

Betty looks at the man who has crawled out of the hole, his liver-spotted face turning to her as she begins to speak. "Can my son go inside to use the…?"

"Nope," says the digger. "Water's off, and we cut the sewer line." Leaning on his shovel, resting what's left of a younger man's muscles under his wrinkled, sunburned arms, the old man seems pleased to have been able to say this to Betty in order to become a player in the comedy he's been watching.

Aida looks again into the hole where she can see an eight-inch-wide cast-iron pipe that has been cut a couple of feet from where it extends out of the soil. Between the cut-off edge of the pipe and the foundation of the house, there is nothing but empty space and a saucer-sized cave in the concrete of the basement wall where a new sewer pipe will go. Aida gets the picture and points into the hole.

"Make him come over here," she says to her daughter-in-law.

Angie looks at his grandmother. "Huh?"

"*What*, Ma?" Betty says, really not understanding.

"In the hole," Aida says. She turns toward the boy. "Nobody sees you." Of course Aida is lying when she says this.

"But I gotta go number *two*," the boy says again.

Aida nods, snaps open the purse she's been carrying, a small valise really, the size and industrial black of an anvil. She knows the bag so well she doesn't have to look in it to find the crumpled, tobacco-flecked tissues at the bottom. Catching a whiff of tobacco as she opens the purse, she could go for a cigarette right now, Aida could.

"Here," Aida reaches out and hands the wad of tissues to Angie. "You go in. You wipe yourself." Angie looks at his mother for help.

"Ma . . . wait . . ." Betty says.

"Okay, I put him in." Unceremoniously, Aida leans over and grabs her grandson under the armpits, lifting him three or four inches off the ground before swiveling to put him in the ditch. The boy winces as Aida lets go of him. It causes her to think back on how much it used to hurt when her father grabbed her under her own armpits, pinching the flesh near her breast buds when she was in his path and he needed to get to work or, worse, to go out and get drunk. This is nothing, Aida thinks, what I'm doing to the boy. He should only know.

But Angie would beg to differ. "Mommy," he implores, looking up terrified.

Betty, for her part, seems hardly able to speak. "Oh, Angie," she says, her eyelids fluttering at the sight of her six-year-old standing in a hole. "You're down there now, just do it."

The boy looks from his mother to his grandmother and back again.

"You want *me* to pull you pants down?" Aida starts to bend toward the hole.

"No!" the boy yells and without wasting another movement yanks down his khaki shorts, underwear along with them. Bending his legs at the knees, he squats and begins to grunt.

Having staged this scene for the audience of men milling near the house, Aida imperiously turns her back on her grandson. Betty has already turned away and Aida makes Tina turn away too. Having complied with her wishes, the boy deserves his privacy.

Except that she is still glancing at him sideways. She's listening for the tinkle of his water and the soft *thush* of his crap hitting the ground. At the angle she is standing, Aida can see the top of Angie's head as he leans forward to bear down harder, his cowlick tickling that place where the top of the house's foundation meets the first row of wooden planks. That's when Aida hears the drone of insects colliding with the sounds of her grandson's eliminations.

The first hornet circles the boy before flying downward into the pit. Two more hornets—awakened in their nest under the house's planks—fly out and follow the first down toward the shit. The boy, with his eyes closed, straining with the muscles in his groin, doesn't become aware of the hornets until one of them swipes past his ear on its way down to the growing pile of waste. Angie opens his eyes, sees the third hornet darting past and howls. The hornets, sensing danger from the gyrating flesh above them, rise from Angie's dung toward the unblemished cheeks of his butt.

The hornets' wings flick his backside; Angie howls again, this time louder, deeper. At the same time, Betty, Tina and the men in the yard all turn to look. It's Aida, however, who first steps back into her role of grandmother-in-charge as soon as Angie starts to swat at the insects.

When the stinging begins Aida already knows she could be blamed for the way this has played out, and she immediately tries to control the damage. She speaks now to Angie in theatrically loud and endearing tones, slipping into Italian.

"*Nonna, fa niente* . . . no move."

Angie swats and swats again, not listening to Aida.

And now she knows that *she's* also going to have to be the one to save the boy. She can see that her daughter-in-law is not going to be any good in this situation. Look at her over there next to the bare-chested men and the digger, all of them frozen in place.

Hiking her skirt, Aida squats like a woman about to give birth in a field. Plunging her arms into the hole, she drags her grandson out by his neck and shoulders, the boy's shorts, underwear and flimsy sandals bumping and scraping off against the jagged edge of the pit.

Lifting Angie into the air, his thin penis flapping, Aida carries the boy away from the hole. He is whimpering and at first Aida doesn't know where to put him down. "Let *me* take him, Ma," says Betty.

But Aida ignores her daughter-in-law, executing a hard left around her and heading toward a door leading to a dark hallway at the back of the house. Skittering, she yells over her shoulder, "I clean him up. He gonna be okay." Then she maneuvers the boy into the hall and kicks the door closed with the toe of her shoe.

Act III

The hallway is dark. Still, the boy's naked rump shines like a moon, picking up what daylight there is from the small windows at the top of the door. Aida drops him onto the floor with his legs in the air. Does she feel shame and compassion and fear added to her guilt when she finally gets a good look at the archipelago of stings pillowing under the skin of her grandson's bottom? Yes. She does. Despite the armor that she has built up around her heart, in this shadowy place Aida feels all of those emotions.

Tightening her jaw, Aida makes eye contact with her grandson and then looks down at the stings. "*Bacci,*" Aida whispers, trying to compose herself. "They kisses. That's all."

The boy exhales an extended, toy-like squeal. In his hand he is desperately clenching the tissues Aida gave him, and she is reluctant to take them from him. Their softness seems to be giving him some kind of comfort. It would be wise to let the boy have this comfort, but she has to do what she has to do.

Prying open her grandson's fist, Aida pulls out the tissues and starts to wipe him. Again, the boy begins to cry. She finishes fast and then backs up. She wants to get the boy on his feet and out of the hallway as fast as she can.

And yet, there is something about the way he is still crying that makes her stop to take a better look at his face. She squints at the wailing *O* of his lips, his crumpled forehead, the flash of his eyes. It's then she notices that Angie's crying face has lost its boyishness. Through pain, his face appears to have become more girlish. Strange, she thinks. Disturbing. There, in front of her in the gloom, is a boy and a girl all in the same face. She analyzes this shaded, genderless face and, as she does something breaks through the thick wall of intervening memories that have been holding it back.

A long, long time ago Aida did not notice or care about the differences between the sexes. Could this memory be real? Little Aida, not much more than a baby, running barefoot alongside a wooden fence, chasing a goat for the pleasure it brought her, seeing her sisters laughing and not recognizing them as girls or boys, watching her older brother lazing on a crooked stone wall but not caring that he is a sex other than hers, looking at her mother and father on the porch but not looking at them as a man or woman, only looking to understand who might comfort her if she stumbled, and who might not. Where did she go, Aida thinks, that little creature?

And now what is *this* feeling? Sadness? *Jesu Cristo.* A *flood* of sadness . . . no, a *lifetime* of sadness covered by rage, beginning for her the moment when men became men and women became women. All she is trying to do in this hallway is help her grandson, to clean him up, and now all this. Where is it coming from?

Aida looks at her grandson weeping on the floor and raises her hand above the boy's body, letting her palm fall onto his breastbone. She is not trying to soothe *him*; she is trying to relieve herself, to flush out this stream of sorrow. Angie catches his breath, closes his eyes, sobs more softly, and Aida presses her hand harder into his chest until he is completely quiet. All this does nothing, however, to silence the disquiet in Aida's own chest. If anything, it is turning into panic.

"What?" Angie has opened his eyes and is staring up in horror at his grandmother's slack face, gone white as a shroud.

Aida looks at him, startled by his voice.

"Nothing," she croaks with a dry throat.

But Angie is not listening. He sits upright with a jolt and starts to cry again, this time louder than before.

Knowing that she'd better get herself together and quickly, Aida rises from the floor onto her creaking knees. She reaches back and flings open the hallway door, having chosen to confront rather than explain. Shading her eyes, she turns to face the light.

"What happened, Ma? Is he okay?" Betty is standing at the saddle of the door and when the boy hears his mother's voice, his sobbing turns into a whimper. Soon it becomes less than that. He's anticipating his mother will save him.

Aida rises from her crouch and stage whispers into her daughter-in-law's ear. "Let him alone. He's acting like a baby."

Scanning the yard, Aida notices her granddaughter. Tina has been sitting sidesaddle on the back seat of the Rambler, the car door open, kicking her bare legs out of boredom. She works to catch Aida's gaze and when she does, she smirks conspiratorially, hoping they can share in the joy of her brother's humiliation. But Aida has nothing for her. What gesture or words could Aida use to teach her this thing about men and women? You can only learn through living.

Interrupting this silent exchange, the digger appears in front of Aida and Betty with the boy's clothes in his hand. Before Betty can stop her, Aida grabs the sandals, short pants and underwear and slides them into the hallway toward her grandson on the floor. When Betty moves forward to help her son, Aida stops her.

"No."

"Mom, he's a little boy."

But as Betty is saying this Angie is already crawling up onto his hands and knees to get dressed. Aida turns from her grandson to the old digger to the formerly bare-chested young men across the yard, both of them having replaced their shirts now.

"That's right," Aida says softly, squinting back at Angie in the hallway. "Put on your pants. Be a man."

WE NOW CONCLUDE OUR BROADCAST DAY

It's Thursday evening, and so far tonight Angelo Santorelli has been in the company of The Flying Nun, Jonathan Winters, and Steve McGarret from *Hawaii Five-0*. Angelo has enjoyed hanging out with all of them, but if he had to pick one to tell his secrets to, he'd pick Steve McGarret. Angelo knows that Steve is the kind of guy who'd understand his lust for Elizabeth Montgomery on *Bewitched*. This wouldn't be something he could share with Joe Friday from *Dragnet*— the guy's too much of a straight arrow to fuck a witch.

Now, after having returned from a commercial break, Angelo is singing along with Dean Martin on *The Dean Martin Show*. Dean's guests tonight have been Raquel Welch, impressionist David Fry and Lou Rawls. They've all been entertaining but at this moment Angelo pictures himself alone on stage with Dean, sharing the spotlight in a little musical number they threw together. Angelo is doing his best to crack Dino up.

Outside this fantasy, Angelo knows he's not really on TV with Dean. He's not a mental patient, for Christ sake. But he *could* be up there, if things had turned out a little differently in his life. A little better. Okay, a lot better. It could be him up there sharing the billing with Raquel.

"Daddy?"

God damn it. Angelo's chubby six-year-old daughter Tina has materialized in the living room clad in her brother's hand-me-down pajamas. Angelo knows what Dino would do with this. He can almost hear Dino deadpanning to the audience.

"Your night to babysit, Pally?"

Big laugh from the studio audience.

Ignore her, Dean.

"Daddy?"

"What, what, what?"

"I'm ascared."

"Where's your mother?" Angelo mumbles.

"In bed. We all fell asleep. I had a dream."

Jesus Christ, kid, all of us have dreams.

"If I let you stay up with me will you be quiet and try to go back to sleep?"

She nods her head.

"Alright lie on the couch."

She shakes her head *no.*

"I want to sleep with you in your chair."

Before Angelo can object, his daughter is already curling up in his lap like a shrimp, sucking her thumb and falling back to sleep.

So Angelo tries to ignore the snuffle of his daughter's breathing to see if he can get back into Dino's good graces. But Dino has moved on. Over there at *The Dean Martin Show,* Lou Rawls has taken over, and he and Dino are hacking it up, taunting Angelo with their inside Hollywood jokes.

All his life Angelo has been *a nobody.* He's got no hidden talents, no special skills. He's not particularly blessed with good looks, or street savvy, or the ability to make money like his brothers, nor is there anything much to distinguish him from any other joker walking the streets trying to get by with nothing more than a haircut and a shoeshine. Everyone either puts him down or simply ignores him. But these people who have risen to the level of stardom on TV, if he could hang out with them, be one of them, somehow, that would be something.

Once Angelo got to shake the hand of each and every member of Sinatra's Rat Pack. Angelo's kid brother, a New Haven city cop, had been assigned to guard the penthouse elevator at the Hyatt Regency where Frank and Dino, Sammy Davis, Jr. and even Joey Bishop and Peter Lawford had camped out before a show at the Shubert Theater. Gino had tipped Angelo off that if he came down and stood in the lobby at the right time, he would be able to catch a glimpse of them. So Angelo was there when the elevator doors opened and out stepped

Frank and the crew. "Mr. Sinatra . . . Mr. Martin . . . Mr. Davis . . ." Angelo tumbled forward, head bowed, holding out his right hand. "I'm so honored. I'm such a fan." He got his handshakes and right then his life changed. The wild possibility of catching another little spark of celebrity that Angelo could kindle into a flame of identity is keeping him alive now. It might never happen again, but somehow it's what gets him through the day. A guy can dream, can't he?

His daughter fully asleep on his lap, Angelo feels the pressure of her weight, and it only makes him more pissed off at the pressure they're all putting on him: his wife, his kids, those shit heads at the machine shop who keep him on piecework and in fear for his job. Jesus Christ, Dean Martin doesn't have to put up with that kind of pressure—Dino coasts through the world with a drink in his hand and a broad on his arm, keeping his wife and kids hidden from view in a house up in Beverly Hills, telling the NBC television network to go fuck themselves if they don't like the fact that he's taking a month off to play Vegas, or just plain play.

Angelo lowers his eyes and sees his daughter's thumb slip from her mouth. Air rushes in over her soft palate and she begins to snore, a baby snore. How deeply and how much like a fully formed, real person she is as she sleeps in his lap. He thrusts out his legs and digs the heels of his stocking feet into the floor, letting Tina gently roll off of him onto the carpet, a few inches at a time, guided only a little by his hands. She does not wake up. What did he do to deserve this kind of trust? What would his kids make of it if they found out he'd rather be spending his time with Dino? For a fraction of a second, this thought thrills him to the hairy edge of mania before plunging him into despair.

Suddenly the room feels darker to Angelo even with the bright colors of Dino's sign-off spot—beautiful girls dressed in purple and green cocktail dresses glide Dean onto a chrome stool where, in between comic thank-yous to his guests, Dino sings.

"Everybody loves somebody sometime . . . Everybody falls in love somehow . . ."

Angelo stands and moves to a place between his daughter and the TV set. What he envisions then both thrills and terrifies him.

From behind the TV, as the credits roll on *The Dean Martin Show*, Angelo imagines that both Sally Fields and Elizabeth Montgomery are creeping out into the living room toward him. He pictures Sally taking off her winged wimple and Elizabeth doffing that inverted ice-cream cone of a witch's hat. Giggling and cackling, they seductively toss their headgear onto the floor at Angelo's feet, shaking out their hair.

"Quiet," Angelo whispers. Though he knows what is real and what is not, he can't tell if he's saying this to Sally and Liz or to his own unquiet mind.

Now it's Friday night, and Angelo hasn't been able to get the TV set to turn back on. He's worked a full shift and an hour of overtime and here he is kneeling on the floor of the living room behind the set, the pressboard backing unscrewed, looking for a burnt-out tube. He's never fixed a TV before, but he's handy enough and he's going to fix this one because there's no money to buy a new set and without it—without TV and the promise of being able to pretend he's someone other than who he is—he might put a gun to his head.

Scanning the miniature landscape of tubes and resistors inside the diorama of the set, what's gnawing at Angelo more than anything else right now is that he's only recently managed to pay it off. This was the cheapest color model he could get his hands on. And getting even this off-brand set was a battle, his wife all the while telling him they had no business buying it what with his punch-the-clock existence. Betty, with her obsession for shopping lists, her over-the-top fondness for what she learned in high school home economics and the prescheduled intercourse she surrenders to once a month in a dark room, had no idea how much getting this set meant to him.

Angelo clips his fingertips onto a tube that appears to be a little dark and wiggles it like a loose tooth. What in God's name did they do to this set while he was at work today? Soap Operas, *Looney Tunes*, Bozo the fucking Clown: what the hell did they watch and how long did they watch it for? More to the point, what did they do while they were watching it? He came into the living room still in his work clothes to get a little overture of news, weather, and sports before his full song and dance with the celebrities of the Friday night programming he loves so much—Tom Jones on *This Is Tom Jones,* not to mention Don Rickles on that show of his the network gave him—and the poor set wouldn't blink.

"Betty," Angelo cries, his head half-inside the set, eyes squinting at the potentially dead tube. "Did somebody do something to this set they weren't supposed to do?"

"Are you coming in for dinner? It's getting cold. The kids are hungry."

Betty says this and a second later Angelo hears her footsteps beating a path toward him.

"I'm not moving from here until I figure out what's wrong with this set," Angelo yells.

"For Christ sake," says Betty. "For once I'd like to see my kids eat their dinner on time."

Her kids. Her dinner. Her schedule. When does he get to play by *his* rules?

"Did somebody bump into it," Angelo calls. "Were the kids playing around it? Tell me."

Angelo can sense Betty a few feet in front of him now, her eyes staring into the convex screen of the picture tube, tapering her scorn through its glass funnel directly into his face.

"I'm hungry, Daddy." It's Tina now. She's joined her mother in the living room. "You always say you're coming to dinner, and we always have to wait for you."

"What did you guys do to the set, Tina?" Angelo's got the tube out and he can see that it truly is bruised black and blue, threaded with a stain of smoke.

"We didn't do anything," Angelo's son Angie calls out from the kitchen.

"It was you, wasn't it, Angie?" Angelo yells.

"Huh?" Angelo hears a chair scrape against the kitchen linoleum and then leather school shoes squeaking toward the living room. "What?"

"Don't lie to me."

This is his boy, his namesake, his only living son—the boy he got as a booby prize after his first son died at birth, a dead son he's fantasized would have been athletic, brave and clever and nothing like Angie. Angelo is so disappointed that Angie is not the son he should have had, he sometimes can't even stand to watch the kid grow up. It's not so much the mistakes that his son makes that bother Angelo, more who Angie *is*. Racing home from school, sneaking TV instead of doing homework, hiding in the basement surrounded by darkness while reading books in the yellow circle of a single naked bulb, living in his head more than his body. Angelo is wise enough to know that he has to couch his frustration with his son in stern reprimands and punishments that appear to be for the kid's own good. He would never admit how much it pains him to see his kid growing up to be an ineffective and dreamy nobody.

"Get over here, Angie."

Angelo rises up from the back of the set with the tube in his hand to find that Angie is not moving.

"Don't make me come over there."

The boy takes a half step back behind his mother. Betty is wearing the dress Angelo was forced into buying her when he forgot her birthday a couple of months ago. Of course she'd be wearing that dress tonight of all nights. She knew the set was broken and wearing that particular dress is her way of reminding him that he's fucked up a thing or two of his own over time.

Angelo crosses from around the back of the set into the middle of the living room where he suddenly stops. He was going to walk all the way to his son, to grab the kid by the neck and make him take a look at the tube, but when he got to the center of the room something came over him. This audience of his family watching him to find out what he'd do next. It put him on stage. For once he feels he has some real power over them, and that gives him pause to stand firm on his mark. He clears his throat.

"This," he begins, holding the tube a bit below his eyeline, "is the tube that you popped when you smashed into my set." He pauses for effect. "And you did smash into this set, didn't you?"

"He did, Daddy," Tina blurts out, her voice trembling. "I told him not to jump around. He was pretending he was inside the TV with the Road Runner."

"Shut up." Angie whacks his sister on the back.

"Don't you hit her," says Angelo.

Betty, who Angelo can see is exhausted, steps away from her son, exposing him to his father. Betty has done her own share of magical thinking about their dead son; Angelo knows that she too would have liked to have that son be this one. He's also smart enough to know that's not quite what's going on here. When Betty crosses her arms and glares at Angelo, he can see that, though it's their clumsy, second son who's disabled the set, she is going to find a way to blame it on Angelo.

"I'm sorry, Dad." Angie whispers this looking at the floor.

"Do you know what this set cost me?" Angelo asks his son, revving up the speech he has been preparing in his head. "It cost me hours and hours of work. And now I have to spend my night without it, trying to figure out a way to fix it." Angelo can't believe how powerful this monologue is making him feel, as if he's been endowed with the magnetism of a celebrity. Liking it, he doubles down by adding a quiver to his voice.

"Here's the worst part," he continues mournfully. "You didn't care about what I had to do to get this set or what it might do to me if you broke it. Well . . . after I fix it, if I ever see you in here playing around this set of mine again, I will make sure you never watch another TV program for as long as you live in this house."

"I'm sorry, Daddy." The kid is panicking now. "I'll help you fix it. I'll pay for it. I promise."

"No," says Angelo. "I don't want your help. And I don't want your money."

Angelo glances from his son to Betty, who appears to be trying to avoid his gaze, no more glares or accusing faces. She can't look him in the eye after the speech he gave. This pleases Angelo no end. The scene with his son has played out so perfectly that he has to remind himself how inappropriate it would be for him to take a bow.

*

Angelo spends most of the rest of the night in his car driving to and from the Boston Post Road—that stretch of Milford, Connecticut highway jammed with furniture, discount, and appliance stores that stay open late. Angelo's going to find a place to sell him the tube and he's going to get home to put it in the set in the hopes of fixing it in time to watch a few minutes of Carson. If he's lucky, he might be able to hang out on the couch with Johnny and his coterie of guests—Lola Falana, and Glen Campbell, Steve McQueen, and Flip Wilson. Angelo looked at the *TV Guide* before he left home to see who'd be on *The Tonight Show*, if only to give himself something to come home for.

Now, up ahead, over the hood of his Nash Rambler, Angelo spies an appliance store with its lights on. It's a big one too—a whale of an enterprise—taking up half a shopping plaza. He knows they've got every tube and TV part ever made stacked in the aisles of that warehouse behind the showroom. His heart beats faster.

He enters the lot and parks the car. Jogging across the blacktop in deepening twilight, he almost knocks over a woman and her kids who are meandering in front of him. "Excuse me, lady." She and the kids watch him as he darts past, and he gets a sense of how pathetically needy he must look clutching his TV tube in his fist.

Reaching the plate-glass storefront that stretches across the lot, Angelo marches past the inside display of washers and dryers, wall ovens, vacuum cleaners, and refrigerators. Before he reaches the double doors to go inside, he spies a single item in a mock living room display. It is a beatific, Godly thing for Angelo, that Magnavox console TV he spies behind the window in the store: French provincial cabinet, solid state (no tubes for your kids to bust), *Chromotone* ("adds vivid depth to color"), a sweet little remote control and, on top of everything else, there's a stereo turntable and AM/FM/Shortwave radio built into the console's tabernacle.

The price on the front of the set nearly makes Angelo weep—six hundred and fifty dollars, over one month's pay before taxes. He needs to get away from this temptation before he does something stupid like try to buy the set using that credit card he's signed up for. But just when he's got it beat he sees something on the screen of the set that makes his heart jump. He sees himself.

It's not a trick of his mind this time; it's actually him in living color, gawking at the screen. Angelo turns his face a little to the left to make sure that what he is looking at is real. He turns his face to the right. He gets curious and looks up to find the camera mounted above the living room display on a pole pointed at the window—a portable color camera, the first of its kind he's ever seen. Slowly he lets his chin drop, giving the set a fulsome smile. Man, if he doesn't look good on TV. He's a handsome guy, after all, even if he is balding a little, even in that worn-out Eisenhower jacket he's still wearing all these years after being mustered out of Korea. He looks younger than he thought he might too: his baby-blue eyes, his flesh smooth, the stubble on his chin and cheeks making him look a little rugged. Yes, he's a bit hunched, but he can fix that.

He pulls back his shoulders, clenches the muscles in his butt and sucks in his stomach. This is *him*. There he is on TV, for real and for true. Come on, Dean, let's sing a song. Hey there, Don, let me show you how to zing the perfect comic insult. Come over here, Lola, and let's make mixed-race magic on *The Tonight Show* tonight.

Angelo takes the tube and stuffs it into the pocket of his jacket, buttoning the flap down tight. His shoulders jerked back, his blue eyes widening, as he enters the store.

Angelo is home the next afternoon when the store delivers the Magnavox. He was supposed to work six or seven hours at the shop. It would have been double time, but he called in sick because he was too excited not to be waiting at home when they brought in the set and he turned it on for the first time. He didn't tell Betty or the kids he'd bought it. Maybe that was a mistake. But it's too late now, because here comes the truck.

When the doorbell rings, his kids come running. Seeing what's being lugged out of the back of the rig by the two deliverymen, Angelo Junior and Tina begin to squeal. Which brings Betty into the front hallway.

"What is this?" she asks.

"Hold on, hold on . . . don't get excited," Angelo says.

"Did you buy this?"

"That's usually how it's done," says Angelo, trying to wisenheimer his way out of this.

"We cannot afford this . . . We cannot pay for this."

"I'll come up with the money," Angelo says. "I'll pay for it."

"No you won't," says Betty. "*We'll* pay for it. The kids and me, like we always do."

Angelo isn't sure what Betty means, but before he can figure it out she shuffles the kids into the kitchen to pick up her purse and the car keys.

"You want us to set this up for you?" the smaller and older of the deliverymen says.

"Yeah, yeah, I guess so." Angelo runs to the kitchen in time to look out the window and see Betty getting into the car with the two kids. "Betty," Angelo calls, opening the back door. "Where're you going?" He steps out the door. "Get back here."

But Betty's got the Rambler rolling down the driveway with his kids fidgeting in the back seat and there's no way he can stop her. Or maybe he's too weak to try.

She has to know how much he loves her. And the kids, don't they know he's given up everything to have them—every fucking thing there was for him to have and to hope for? He'd do anything for them, and all he wants in return are his fantasies.

"You want us to take away the old set?" The younger deliveryman is calling to Angelo from the living room.

His head hanging, Angelo walks the hallway toward the men setting up the Magnavox.

"Yeah, take it away," he says.

The Magnavox console has been plugged in, wired to Angelo's outside aerial and ready to emit life. It's a behemoth and Angelo stares at it in awe.

The deliverymen lift Angelo's wounded set from the floor and hoist it into the heavy cardboard case the Magnavox arrived in. The old set is so much tinier than the new console that it swims there, drowning in a box twice its size. Before they get it out the door, Angelo gets a feeling that he too is in over his head.

It's Saturday night and so far this evening Angelo Santorelli has been in the company of Jackie Gleason, Johnny Cash, and a bevy of A-list royalty on *The Hollywood Palace:* Jimmy Durante, Louis Armstrong, Chita Rivera and Sugar Ray Robinson, all guided by this week's host, Sammy Davis Jr. Inching up to eleven p.m., there's no sign of Angelo's wife and kids. Maybe they're staying with her sister or her mother. Wherever they are, Angelo has tried to keep his spirits up by pretending to trade pratfalls with Jackie Gleason on *The Jackie Gleason Show* and imagining himself in a musical medley on *The Johnny Cash Show.*

The truth is that the Magnavox is a beast of a TV. The wattage and picture quality are beyond belief, but sitting in front of it for nearly four hours, Angelo is beginning to wonder if it hasn't taken over his life more than it should for a man in his situation. His wife and kids have left and, with the set holding him hostage, he hasn't yet summoned the will or swallowed the pride to go out and find his family to bring them back.

"I'd like to thank my guests: Miss Chita Rivera, my man Sugar Ray Robinson . . ." Inside the set, Sammy Davis Jr. is saying his goodnights on *The Hollywood Palace.* The entertainer is surrounded by his guest stars. "Mr. Jimmy Durante, and, of course, my hero, Louis 'Satchmo' Armstrong."

Angelo rises from his chair, walks to the TV and kneels in front of it as if it were an altar. He brings his face close to the screen, scrutinizing Louis's yellow teeth and purple gums. Squinting sideways, he can see Sammy's glass eye staring at him wildly; Jimmy Durante's mushroom cluster of a nose; Chita Rivera's caked foundation makeup; two scars above Sugar Ray Robinson's left eyebrow. Why does Angelo feel so tired? So much more tired than he's ever felt in his life?

He tilts off his knees, lays his shoulder on the floor and closes his eyes. Fading. Drifting. As he does he hears something behind him. In his head, he spins around to see Betty, maybe, but not . . .

Chita Rivera?

He could be dreaming but what a dream: Chita Rivera in his living room, legs for miles, fishnet stockings and décolletage packed into a bustier. Striking a pose, Chita crooks her finger at Angelo before vamping toward the Magnavox where Sammy Davis Jr. and the rest of his guest stars are waiting inside.

Take me with you. Angelo can hear himself.

Chita smiles and cocks her head and when Angelo looks back at the screen of the Magnavox he finds that the luminaries from *The Hollywood Palace* have been joined by every other TV entertainer and celebrity that he has ever fantasized about being or being with. There's Dean Martin—booze and cigarette in hand, Johnny Carson and Jackie Gleason decked out in midnight-blue tuxes, Lola Falana and Elizabeth Montgomery in flashy sequined couture, Tom Jones, Johnny Cash, Sally Fields and Lou Rawls—on and on and on—all inside the set waiting.

Angelo smiles. It's all coming together for him now. He's finally going to be who he's wanted to be.

But when he reaches out for Chita's hand, she disappears in a puff of white light to reemerge back inside the set.

I want to come in, Angelo whispers at the screen.

Dean Martin begins to laugh and the rest of the stars follow suit.

Studying this chortling lineup of entertainers, Angelo again sees the scars, the glass eye, the makeup hiding the blemishes of declining years, all of it pronounced and freakish—nearly unbearable to look at.

Their laughter rising now, Angelo realizes with a jolt that it's meant for him. They know he wants to be one of them. And they're laughing at him because he already *is* one of them, scared and aging and human as hell. And then . . .

A military band strikes up the "Star Spangled Banner." It is coming from inside the Magnavox, wiping the laughter from the screen.

Someone has pulled a fast one on Angelo. He can feel it in the crater of his subconscious. Exhausted, he wants the anthem to stop and just then a cymbal crashes and the music is brought to a close.

He opens his eyes.

The room around him is empty, not a celebrity in sight, on screen or off. Angelo, his head on the floor, blinks. Inside the set, an American flag is waving at him vertically, tricking him into thinking it can wave in a direction it was never meant to wave.

"WTNH, New Haven now concludes its broadcast day."

He lies motionless and listens to the drone of the announcer. He's a man no one ever sees and now he's telling Angelo that he has overstayed his welcome. The programming he loves so much is finished; the celebrities he wants to be have left and will not be returning.

It's time for Angelo to get up off the floor and go to bed. He'll stop by his son's room to stare at Angie's empty pillow, chasing back the thought of how much he dislikes and fears for his son because of how much he dislikes and fears for himself. Then he'll peek into Tina's room where he'll picture his body lying in Tina's empty bed, having just come out of his own bad dream, afraid and longing for a father to comfort *him*. When he gets into his own bed, Angelo will pull the covers over his head, and then he'll be alone with himself and no one else for the first time in a long time.

In a moment, he'll do all of this. First he'll have to pry himself away from the whining, circular test pattern inside the Magnavox, that symbol of American emptiness broadcasting the false promise that tomorrow will be a better day. Another chance to become someone he can never hope to be.

VALIANT

A couple of weeks after my first year in boarding school ended with me nearly getting put in jail, my father stepped into the den to talk with my sisters and me. I was in there lying on the floor with coconut-sized headphones covering my ears, listening to Pink Floyd's *The Dark Side of the Moon.* My sisters Allegra, Sophia, and Isabella were watching a *Charlie's Angels* rerun on one of the four new nineteen-inch Sony Trinitrons my father had bought my mother, Angela, the Christmas before, telling her to sprinkle them around the house in various rooms of her choosing.

The military boarding school my father had sent me to in Virginia after he'd gotten fed up with my antisocial antics and failing grades had given me time to think about how to steal a large amount of cash from him. I was sixteen years old and, unbeknownst to my father, devising unscrupulous ways to get money was what he had taught me best. Among other things, that night in the music room I was putting the finishing touches on a *Mission Impossible*-style heist I'd pull off to get at the money I was sure he had locked somewhere in his filing cabinet or desk on the third floor.

"All of you, listen up," my father said, entering the room.

I was a little high from the joint I had smoked out in the woods at the edge of our property a couple of hours earlier. I could see his lips moving and hear his words through the music, but I felt no desire to listen to what he had to say. My sisters, likewise, were taken with watching Farrah Fawcett kick some poor guy's ass. They, too, saw no reason to register my father's presence. We were all long past the ages where we worried about what he might do to us if we ignored him. What could he do, we figured, throw us out of the house? My mother—who also pretended not to hear my father when the mood struck her—would never have stood for it.

My father, wearing his buttoned-up work shirt and Windsor-knotted tie, walked over to the headphone jack and yanked the little penis-shaped plug out of the socket. *The Dark Side of the Moon* exploded into the room, held in by the Italian tapestries my mother had hung on the walls. My father dropped the jack and covered his ears, scrunching up his nose and graying mustache so that his wire-rimmed glasses nearly fell off his face. He had always reminded me of the banker on the Monopoly game, and now he looked like the banker on the Monopoly game being force-marched out of the 1920s and slammed headfirst into a few megadecibels of 1970's rock and roll.

My oldest sister, Isabella, the angriest one, got up from where she sat on a love seat to flip off the stereo. Then she lowered the volume on the TV.

"Why'd you do that?" Isabella asked my father. "We're watching a show."

A puff of uncertainty fogged up my father's eyeglasses. For all his ability to gamble bags of money on real estate, he was not an overly brave man when it came to directly confronting people. He'd much rather pay other people to do it for him. Isabella, the oldest, had been the first to figure this out a couple of years earlier.

"I need to tell you all something," my father said. "Your mother and I have decided that we will no longer be funding the activities and privileges that you all seem to be taking for granted around here."

All four of us stared at him. Neither my sisters nor I thought of ourselves as privileged. We thought of our father's money as payment for having to put up with a man who had mostly treated us as a small workforce he employed as needed. Case in point: The four of us at thirteen, ten, eight and seven years old standing like the von Trapp family on the bedroom staircase being forced to introduce ourselves by name, grade and hobbies to dinner guests my father was trying to impress. Case in point: My father attempting to strong-arm me into getting up at a political fundraiser to give a speech he had written for me to show how the "youngsters" of our city were in favor of the pro-real estate development candidate he was backing.

"Okay fine," said Isabella, "take away our privileges." She reached over to turn the TV back on but my father stepped between her and the set.

"Hey, come on, Dad," Sophia, the youngest one, said. "I want to finish the show."

"What difference does it make?" Allegra, two years older than me, said to Sophia. "He spoiled it now for us anyway."

"I don't think any of you really understand the consequences of what I'm telling you," my father said. "Let me give you some examples."

My father—the son of semi-illiterate, immigrant parents, a man who had worked overtime to forget how dumb and poor they had started out—was turning into an English schoolmaster. This was the role he took on with those he felt were somehow stronger but less intelligent than he.

"Example one," my father turned to Isabella. "You know that horse of yours that we lease so you can flirt with your instructor? Well, that's off the table until your attitude improves."

If this affected Isabella in any way, she didn't show it. She smirked and picked up the *TV Guide*.

"Example two," said my father. He was now looking at Allegra. "I know you're planning on a big shindig out there at the beach club for your birthday. Well, you're welcome to have it, as long as you can figure out a way to pay for it yourself."

"Jesus, Daddy," Allegra whined. "Mommy and I have been working on those invitations for weeks."

"Example three," my father said, turning to Sophia, the easiest mark of all. "You, little girl, have been spending way too much time with those dance classes of yours."

"Daddy, no," said Sophia, the pockets of her eyes filling with tears.

"Let me tell you something, missy," said my father. "Those costumes and recitals are not free, and I will not shell out one more dime until I see you pitching in around here a bit more."

"Daddy, please." Sophia was weeping openly now.

As high as I was I couldn't help seeing the farce in all this, coming, as it had, from a man who once spent a hundred and eighty dollars on a case of imported Italian peaches: perfectly large, rosy pieces of fruit that he'd had my mother dole out to him one at a time from a cool spot in the basement like gold nuggets from a mine. Thinking about the peaches sent me over the edge, and I snickered.

"And you," my father said. "You, Charles, are example four."

I knew what was coming before he said it.

"You know that Camaro you've been begging me to buy you for the last year? Well, you can forget about that until we see some serious improvements in your grades and a much better report from Commandant Clark when you return to boarding school in the fall."

I immediately stopped laughing and began thinking about the criminal ruckus I'd caused the previous year at that boarding school. The times I'd summoned up the nerve to pull open the fire alarm box at three a.m. or broken into the chemistry lab to steal nitrous oxide, or hot-wired the commandant's car to drive it into the middle of the parade ground and leave it there with the doors, hood and trunk open. All of this in a thinly disguised attempt to get myself expelled.

I then began thinking about the plot I'd been hatching since I found out that I *wasn't* going to get expelled. The one where I'd come home to find the thousands in cash I was sure my father had hidden somewhere in his office on the third floor of the house. Uncovering this stash, I'd fit as much of it as I could into a brown supermarket bag, and then I'd buy the Camaro outright and drive off to Canada. It was the one place I believed I could drive to where my father might never be able to get to me.

"Are you done now?" Isabella said to my father. Isabella had stood up to console Sophia, who had her wet face buried in a couch cushion. "You're a prick, you know that?"

My father pretended he hadn't heard her. Isabella shook her head in disgust and then pulled Allegra and Sophia off the couch and out of the room.

I felt some pity for my father, and I looked at him and shrugged as much as to say, "You should have seen it coming." Except that he took it another way.

"Oh, I see that you're too *cool* to let any of this bother *you*, hmm?"

I shrugged again, thinking I'd show him who was cool and who was not when I took off with ten or twenty thousand dollars of his money in a brand new Camaro Z28.

The next afternoon I was at the top of our driveway in front of the detached garage where my father parked his Lincoln, fantasizing about my new 1977 Camaro as I watched Soupy Nardini press his nose into the water pump of a 1962 Plymouth Valiant. Soupy was older than me by almost a year and he was the kid I most wanted to be. He was from a much poorer family and his father was mostly unemployed. But he was freer and more sure of himself than I would ever be.

"Hey Chucky," Soupy called up from under the hood. "Find me a three-eighths socket head."

I walked around to the trunk of the Valiant and started looking in the drawers of Soupy's toolbox. Soupy lived in a small apartment in a slummy part of the city with his mother, father and two brothers. His father and he had towed this car back to their place from Elm City Auto Wrecking and for the past three months Soupy had been working on it on the street in front of his apartment. Now the Valiant was at my house while he worked on it some more.

Opening the lid at the top of Soupy's toolbox, I saw the socket heads lined up in perfect ascending order with an eighteen-inch bolt cutter laid on top of them. I moved the bolt cutter and pulled out the three-eighth-inch socket, walking it to Soupy.

Soupy took the socket head from me, tightened a bolt and walked around the right fender to climb into the driver's seat. Once inside the car, he turned the key and a cannon blast of black smoke erupted from the tailpipe.

Storm clouds of exhaust darkened my driveway as Soupy gunned the car. It was from within this smog that I spotted the silver grillwork of my father's Lincoln creeping up the blacktop. He was home from work early.

I leaned into Soupy through the open door of the car and tapped him on the shoulder.

"He's home!" I yelled over the rising rpm's of the engine.

"What?" Soupy yelled back. He looked at me, switching off the ignition. With the car suddenly shut down, a chill of quiet filled the backyard, a nervous silence pricked by bird chirps and the ticks of warm engine oil.

I waited for Soupy to make eye contact with me, and then I tilted my head in the direction of my father's car. He had parked his Lincoln about ten feet behind Soupy's car and was pulling himself out of the driver's seat. As he did, he called out.

"Mr. Nardini?"

Soupy twisted over the front seat of his car and looked back through the Valiant's rear window toward my father's Lincoln. Seeing that Soupy was not going to get out of his car, my father cleared his throat and called out more harshly.

"Please move your car as soon as possible so I can garage my automobile." My father started toward the house, squinting back at me from under his black eyebrows before he got halfway there.

"And you, Charles," he called over his shoulder, "please see me in the kitchen *now*."

He was gone before I could think of a reply that would show Soupy how I wasn't going to let my father order me around like that.

"I'm outta here," Soupy said. He slid out of the car and closed the hood.

I looked into the open toolbox in the trunk.

"Hey, Soup, you mind if I borrow those bolt cutters?"

"What do you need 'em for?"

"I lost the key to my bike lock," I lied. "I have to cut off the chain."

"Alright, take 'em but you gotta give 'em back. Okay?"

"I will," I said.

I scuffled to the trunk and lifted out the tool. With the bolt cutters in my hand I felt loose and dangerous, a boy holding a weapon.

I closed the trunk and waited for Soupy to drive away. Once he was gone I looked around and then I stuffed the bolt cutters up into one of the down spouts that came off the roof of the garage. With the handles shut, they were the right size to hide perfectly in place until I needed them.

In the kitchen I found my father on the speakerphone with my uncle Eddy. We were the only family I knew back then who had a speakerphone in their house. In fact we were the only family I knew back then who had a phone in every room of their house. My father had hired an electrician to tie them into an intercom system that he could use to talk with anyone anywhere in the house anytime he wanted.

"Eddy, I'm telling you to withdraw that application." My father saw me and snapped his fingers for me to sit down at the table. He had rolled up his sleeves, always a disturbing sight because he never rolled up his sleeves unless something bad was about to happen.

I took my time sitting. As I did, I noticed that his briefcase was open on the tabletop and that a manila folder had been placed in front of the chair where I usually sat.

"You will not use my name as a reference to buy a boat, Edward," my father said into the phone. "You will not use my name as a reference to buy anything whatsoever. You may not have a reputation to protect in this town, but I do."

There were stories I'd heard about my uncle Eddy that tied him to the local mob. My father tried to avoid contact with him but every so often Uncle Eddy would break into my father's crystal palace. I never knew exactly what my uncle did to get his money, but I was pretty sure that whatever he did wasn't much different from the deals my father had worked to get the money to put an intercom in every room and a Lincoln in our three-car garage.

"Yeah, Carlo." My Uncle Eddy's voice came through the speaker box in the wall. "From what I hear, you got quite a reputation to protect. There are bank inspectors all over town looking to get their hands around your reputation."

My father looked at me in a way that said, *You will kindly strike that remark from the record.*

"Thanks anyway, Carlo," crooned Uncle Eddy, sarcasm stitched into the words. "There's more than one way to get a boat."

"I'm hanging up now," my father shouted at the wall.

"So long, Carlo," Uncle Eddy replied. "See you in jail."

Uncle Eddy hung up first. My father walked over and punched a button to kill the drone of the speakerphone's dial tone. The thought of my father going to jail had never occurred to me before. Now that it had, it was all I could think about.

"Please open that folder on the table," said my father.

When I made no immediate motion to do it, he got louder.

"Open it," he repeated.

Pinching the corner of the folder as though I were handling plutonium, I flicked it open. Inside sat a piece of onionskin filled with typewritten characters. I glanced at it. At the bottom was a signature line with my name printed out in full, "Charles Anthony Santorelli Jr."

"What's this supposed to be?" I asked my father. I was pretending that I didn't care, but when I saw that it was something I was going to have to sign, I grew worried. Who knew what my father had cooked up here?

"It's a contract between us," my father said. "You will sign it, agreeing to bring up your grades to a B-plus average. Likewise, you will agree to behave yourself at school in the fall, thereby ending those disturbing phone calls I regularly had to have with the commandant. Should you agree to and meet these terms over the course of a year we will then talk about buying you a car."

My father was a foxy bastard. He knew I'd never be able to hold a B-plus average. I'd never gotten more than a C-minus in any subject I'd ever taken. Someone looking in on this scene might have thought that this contract was a simple strategic incentive, one used by fathers since the beginning of time to focus an unfocused kid. I knew differently. I knew my father. This contract was his way of ensuring he'd never have to spend a dime on a car for me.

"There's no way I'm signing this," I said.

"Suit yourself. But if you don't sign it you will never have any chance of getting that car you want so badly. It will also prove to me that you are exactly the person I thought you were."

That really got to me, and I slammed the folder shut against the table. I pictured my father sitting in that jail cell that my uncle had talked about, and now I was sitting there beside him. The two of us exactly the person the other thought we were. There was no way I was going to let that happen to me, and I slammed the top of the folder again to make sure he knew it.

"You can get angry if you want," said my father, "but it won't help your cause."

I looked at my father. Over his shoulder my three sisters were peeking through a six-inch opening they had made by pushing in one of the café doors between the dining room and the kitchen. Isabella, her face above Allegra's and Sophia's, was making horror-movie faces, mocking my father behind his back. When the other two saw her do it, they started in as well—bulging Saturday-matinee eyes, histrionic hands cupped over their mouths. I looked away from them.

"What about Isabella, Allegra and Sophia? Do they get a contract too?"

My father caught me glancing at the dining room and he whipped around. The girls were too fast for him, however. By the time my father looked, they were gone.

"I will deal with each of them in my own way," my father said.

I stood up from the table and walked around it past my father toward the dining room.

"Don't forget your contract."

He took it off the table and held it out for me. I snatched it with that sixteen-year-old viciousness all my friends used to wither their parent's spine. My father's backbone did not so much as twitch.

When I got to my bedroom, I folded the contract into increasingly smaller squares until it was the size of a Chunky candy bar. I tried to toss it into the wastebasket, but it unfolded in midair, puffing out enough to drag it to a stop somewhere short of the pail.

It had already become a living thing that was out of my control.

The next day was a Saturday and it was raining. I woke up to the sound of water on the roof directly above my head. I slept on the third floor of the house in an unfinished attic room that I'd taken over to get away from the rest of my family who slept on the second floor. The third floor was also where my father kept his office.

"Charlie, are you up?" My mother's voice entered the room from the hallway. By the time I sat up on the single mattress that I'd placed on the floor, she had opened the door and was standing in my room with a mug in her hand.

"I thought you'd like something hot to drink. I made cocoa. It's a terrible day out there."

She walked over to the milk crate I used as a nightstand and put the cocoa on it.

"I wish you'd at least let us move the rest of the furniture up here from your room downstairs. It's embarrassing to see my son sleeping on a mattress on the floor."

"I like it like this," I said, laying back down.

She raised her eyebrows. "You should be careful what you wish for." She pointed to the cup on the milk crate. "Drink your cocoa and get up now, okay?"

She stepped away and her heel landed on the folded contract that had been on the floor since the day before. She picked it up, looked at it for a moment, and then sat on the crate next to my bed, dropping the contract onto the mattress.

"He's only doing what he thinks is right," she said. There was a hitch in her voice. Even she didn't believe what she was saying.

She hadn't yet put on her makeup or combed her hair. She was wearing an old blue bathrobe that had a string of fading silver hearts lining the collar. Even with no more decoration than that, my mother was still pretty.

"He's got some screwed-up thoughts about what's right," I said.

She reached out and brushed back a hank of hair that had fallen across my eyes. Feeling her fingers on my face, I had to stop myself from rolling closer to put my head on her lap. I wanted to give her a reason to run her fingers through the hairs at the base of my neck in the same place she used to when I was little. I needed her to tickle that brush of newly cut hair that was now covered over in unwashed, overgrown curls but used to be there when I lay down next to her at five or six years old at the beach club or on her bed after my bath.

"Okay," she said, getting up from the crate. "Get up now."

"Is he home?" I asked. She stopped and turned toward me but didn't answer. She suddenly looked weary.

"Is he *home*?" I asked again.

"Yes," she said. "He's sleeping." She took a deep breath. "He was up late."

As soon as she said this, I understood that her weariness was not from having to deal with me. It was from having to deal with my father.

"Get up now, Charlie. Please."

She walked out of the room, and I crawled off the mattress and across the floor, kneeling in front of the window, which had been dormered into the roof. I gazed into the backyard. Water was flowing so fast from the downspouts in the garage, it looked like someone had turned on a tap.

Thirty minutes later I was dressed and headed downstairs when I bumped into Allegra on the second floor landing. She was wearing a gauzy cotton peasant blouse through which I could make out the shadowy dark outline of her nipples. I had clobbered the stairs two at a time coming down from the third floor and was trying for an innocent-looking getaway when Allegra hissed at me.

"Shhh . . ." she said. She pointed at the round window over the stairway.

I looked out the eighteen-inch-wide porthole. On the street at the side of the house, slick and shiny in the morning rain, was a white van. Inside the van sat a guy with a beard and a wide-brimmed hat that made him look like a Mexican cowboy. If I had to guess, I would have said that the guy was at least ten years older than Allegra.

She hopped down a step and stood next to me at the window. "If Mommy asks," she whispered, "tell her that I went to the mall with Rosie Franco." I nodded but then Sophia came out of her bedroom and saw us standing on the stairs.

"Where are you going in that shirt?" Sophia said. "Mommy will kill you if she sees you in that."

"Shut up," Allegra said before slipping down the stairs as softly as she could.

Three seconds later I heard the front door quietly open and shut. When I looked out the porthole, Allegra was sprinting through the rain to get into the van. She'd barely closed the door to the van when she and the Mexican cowboy raced off down Edgewood Avenue.

"Daddy's going to find out and lock her in her room," Sophia said.

"Not if you don't say anything." It was Isabella who'd appeared in the doorway of her room. She must have been the one who'd helped Allegra engineer her adventure with that guy in the van. One way or another my three sisters would always help each other escape from my father. That was good for them, I thought. I was on my own.

"Say anything about what?" said my mother. She had come out of the hallway bathroom where she had combed her hair and put on makeup, quite a lot of it, as if she were trying to hide from something.

My sisters and I looked at each other.

"It's nothing," said Sophia. "Allegra went to the mall with Rosie Franco."

I was never courageous as a little boy. If the much-younger me had known what I was on my way to do that morning, he would have run away to hide in a closet or bury himself in the arms of his oldest sister. If you asked me I couldn't have told you where I was getting the courage to carry out the scheme I had hatched, but by then these things had started to come easier and easier to me.

"What the hell are you doing, Charlie?"

I was in the mudroom at the back door off the kitchen and Isabella had spotted me looking for a hooded jacket to shelter my head from the rain. I had just come from the encounter with her and my other sisters on the landing, and I was headed to the garage.

"I'm going out."

"The fuck you are." Isabella swooped in and sandwiched herself between me and the back door. I was in awe of how sure my sister was of her own movements.

"It's pouring out there, you idiot. Get in here." Isabella spun me around, steering me into the kitchen and across the dark marble tile of its floor. When we reached the full-length café doors that led to the dining room, she shoved me through them and into one of the dining room chairs.

"What are you up to?" She towered over me, looking down like a hawk on perch.

"Nothing. It's none of your fucking business."

"*You're* my fucking business."

Sophia walked into the room. She looked at Isabella. "What did he do now?"

"It's none of your fucking business," both Isabella and I said at the same time to Sophia.

"Jesus," Sophia said, "I'm not a baby you know. I know what's going on around here."

"Yeah, what do you know?" I asked her.

"I know that Daddy's losing his mind and he's ready to throw you out."

"Not if I get away first," I said.

That was enough to momentarily stop Isabella and Sophia.

"Did he make *you* sign a contract? Huh, Sophia?" I turned to Isabella. "How about you, did he make *you* sign one?"

They looked at me, shocked to have finally realized that it might only be me, their father's son, who had been doomed by some family edict to fail.

And how much more shocked would they have been if I told them that before I came downstairs I had searched my father's office, dumping the contents of every drawer in his desk and filing cabinets all over the floor until I found the few hundred dollars he kept in there—not the thousands I had expected, but the only money I could find anywhere I had looked? How much more ashamed of herself would Isabella have been about her power to succeed—to help my sisters succeed and escape cleanly—if I let her know that when she had stopped me in the mudroom I was headed out to the garage downspout to get the bolt cutters and snap the battery cables on my father's Lincoln so he couldn't follow me when Soupy Nardini came to pick me up to drive me to the Greyhound station in New Haven?

"Where are *your* fucking contracts?" I asked my two sisters now that I had them cold.

A cabinet door opened and closed in the kitchen. Water ran in the kitchen sink. "Calm down, Carlo," we heard my mother say.

The three of us pivoted toward the full-length café doors. Isabella slid toward the left door and nudged it open a crack so that all three of us could see my mother standing next to my father, who had sat down at the kitchen table.

My father had his face in his hands, his elbows forming a lectern he was using to hold up the weight of his head. Moving his hands, he rubbed his forehead and I could see he wasn't wearing his eyeglasses. He was all but blind without those steel-rimmed spectacles, and the sight of his naked eyes coated with a dull scrim of water made me feel sad in a way I couldn't explain.

"Where are the children?" my father murmured to my mother.

Isabella let the doors close till all but a sliver of space was left between them. Sophia hunkered away from the crack that remained. Me, I felt myself split in half, one part of me quiet behind the crack, the other watching myself run away so I wouldn't have to see my father like this any longer.

"They're somewhere," my mother said. "I don't know. Don't worry about the kids right now." She handed my father a tiny white pill she had shaken loose from a prescription bottle. My father popped it in his mouth and swallowed it with a gulp from a glass of water on the table in front of him.

"It's bad, Angela." My father sniffed, gulping air. "I thought I could cover the loans before it went this far." My mother took his chin and raised his head so that their eyes met. "I made some mistakes, not thinking clearly, not really thinking sharply, I mean … I didn't want to lose everything." He paused. "For you and the kids..."

My mother dropped her hand from my father's chin. Whatever compassion she'd had for him when she looked into his eyes was now completely gone.

I could see my father beginning to burn from having wordlessly been revealed as a liar. His fingers, which had been worrying the sweat off the water glass in front of him, suddenly tightened, and he lifted the tumbler from the table and threw it against the wall. Running down the wall, the water in the glass brought out the red viscera of the pink flowers in the designer wallpaper of which my mother was so proud.

When my father screamed, my sisters and I jumped. My mother, though visibly shaken, held her ground. She was not falling for his rage.

And that was when my father began to break apart, body and soul. His neck muscles became roped and stringy, vibrating and crimson. His mouth opened, begging like a baby bird's beak, shoulders jackhammering, chest heaving, hyperventilating. Then came the sobbing. Sobbing like nobody's business.

Isabella let go of the swinging door, closing up this view of my father. Tough as she was, she couldn't look at it any more either. Sophia had already stopped looking some moments ago and was sitting on the floor against the dining room wall. To me, it didn't matter whether Isabella kept the door open or closed. I was already walking away.

"Where are you going?" Isabella whispered. But I didn't answer her this time, and this time she knew better than to try and stop me.

In the distance I'd heard the blistering cough of Soupy's Valiant closing in on our house. He'd have to wait a minute longer for me now out at the edge of our driveway. I had to go back to the third floor to do something first. I had thought about putting the money back where I found it. But that wasn't it. I was going to keep the money in spite of what I saw.

It was the contract I was going back upstairs for. There was no way I was leaving that contract behind in this house. No way I was going to leave behind that evidence of my failure. No way that I wanted anyone to know that my father had tried in his own imperfect way to show his love for me, and that I had failed to love him in return.

LITTLE MAN

> When you get G.I. Joe you'll have the
> greatest realism, the greatest fun you
> ever had playing soldier . . .
> — Hasbro, 1964

Hey, you.

That's right, you. I'm talking to you, boy. You keep your eyes up here on *me*.

No. No. Not the Slinky. Not the Goddamn Slinky. Mr. *Slinky* is not talking to you, boy. No. Not the Matchbox cars or the Batman and Robin game or the Lincoln Logs. I am not some mother-humping Lincoln Log, sitting over here on this bookcase waiting for you to look at me. It's me, soldier. Me. You put down that paper bag, you put down that airplane glue, you stop what you're doing and you listen to *me*.

Come on now, son, you remember the fun we had killing Japs. Don't you?

Take the jeep and get some ammo, fast.

They got me pinned down. We need reinforcements.

Remember.

I'd talk to you in that voice you made up for me, and then you'd talk back. Let's do that again, boy. Let's kill some Japs for old times' sake. Don't make me beg. Come on, let's have some honest to God, mother-humping fun, like we used to. What do you say?

Goddamn it, that is an order now, boy.

Alright, how about some Cong, boy? How about we kill some Viet Cong? I'd do that with you, boy, I would. I love you that much.

Don't look at me like that, soldier. Pick up your head. Stop peeking up at me like I'm some crazy little man.

Goddamn it, boy. Your father'll kick your ass if he finds you in here like this, your face inside that bag. Do not make me have to go wake up your father to tell him what you're doing.

What? You think you're hallucinating me? You think I'm some drugged-up figment of your imagination?

That's right, boy. You better shake your head *No*. You better Goddamn believe I'm real. I'm real as shit for you, son. I'm Goddamn G.I. Joe. I'm twelve inches of mother-humping U.S. Cavalry and I'm gonna save you if it kills me.

Don't you look away from me, boy. Goddamn it, you stop breathing them fumes out of that bag right now.

That's it—that's right—you turn around and look at yourself in that mirror over there. Take a good look at them dirty, bell-bottom dungarees and that ripped t-shirt. Fifteen years old and that stringy black hair of yours already hanging down in your eyes. What happened to you, boy? What happened to the kid I knew with the clean fingernails and the nice smile, those big brown eyes . . . Little John . . . jumping around in here after basketball practice . . . that kid who used to cheat when he played Monopoly with his cousins . . . the boy who didn't want anybody finding out how he hid under the bed when he got scared . . . that sweet kid who told me dumb jokes?

"Knock, knock." "Who's there?" "Hatch." "Hatch who?" "God bless you."

God, I miss that kid.

Okay, listen, son, I got an idea. Here's what we do. Just like old times. You go in the kitchen, you get yourself a big glass of milk, put in a mess of that Strawberry Quik you used to like so much. Your mother, she'll be on the couch like she always is this time of night, smoking her way through a pack of a Viceroys, drinking, passing out before the end of *Bonanza*. She won't even notice you. She never does any more. So you go grab that milk and a sack a Twinkies and come back here. I'll get the blankets out of the closet to make us some sand dunes, stack up some shoeboxes for bunkers, lay down that blue bath towel we used to pretend was the ocean. We'll build ourselves a beachhead.

We'll get Navy Frog Man and Air Force Pilot Joe outta the footlocker, Camouflage Marine Joe too. We'll prop up a few of them enemy Joes, the German ones, the Nazis, all tricked up in their swastikas, their Iron Eagles, clawing at their grenades and burp guns. We'll roll in with the jeep and the searchlight, the Higgins Boat, all the accessories —tiny guns, little helmets, scale-model belts and canteens. We'll take it *all* out, every last piece of mother-humping G.I. Joe equipment we got—the whole arsenal—and we'll fight D-Day all over again.

Hit the beach . . . Take the hill . . . Frag that town, soldier . . . Kill 'em all!

How about that, boy, that sound like fun?

Oh for Christ sake, boy, don't lie down on the floor now. Don't close your eyes. Don't pass out. Wake up. Look at me, son . . . tell Joe what's bothering you.

Come on. Come on. You don't think I know what you been through, boy? You don't think I understand. I've been here with you since 1964, for God's sake—first year they made me, first year *you* made me real—you just eight years old. I understand. Your mother and father always putting themselves first—Eddy and Rita, Rita and Eddy—your father a too-proud Italian trying to hide that the work he does for the unions is the work of a criminal, your mother putting on airs and pretending she isn't a criminal's wife, hypocrites both of them and neither of them much good at being parents either, more interested in their clothes, their hairdos, their rec room, their kitchen, their cars in the driveway than they are in you, feeding you and giving you a place to live, sure, but not much else, screaming curses at you when you did something they didn't like—mud on your pants, math homework you couldn't figure out how do, a whiney mouth instead of a smile when they told you to sit up straight, eat your dinner, turn off the TV, stop acting like a baby. And through it all shoving toys at you, thinking that would be enough to keep you happy in the land of the free and home of the brave.

But you never were that happy, and you never were that brave. Were you, boy? I seen your father smacking you around behind this bedroom door when he didn't like how scared you got over little things, afraid you'd turn out to be a sissy, trying to toughen you up, he said, beating you for your own good to make you into a man, as if beating your son was the only way a man could show his love and being a man was the only thing worth being. All the while you thinking you were a worthless coward. Hating him and your mother too for who they were and what they did to you, and you not being able to do a damn thing about it. Hating the world for being this world. Hating yourself for being this weak.

I get it, son. But we gotta fight now. You hear? Right now. Snap to, boy. You got that fightin' spirit inside you. I know you do. Show us what America's made of—greatest power on earth; nothing we can't do; no country greater than ours. You know the drill.

That's it, kid. Get up off the floor. Claw your way on over here. Attaboy. I knew you had it in you. Good boy . . .

Don't stop there now, son, keep going. Why'd you stop? What are you looking for under that bookcase? Get your face off the floor right now.

Whoa boy . . . what are you doing with a full-size 45 automatic under there? You know the regulations, boy: "Official G.I. Joe gear must not exceed one-sixteenth actual size; weapons and other field equipment must be . . ."

Sweet Jesus, kid! Don't go pointing that pistol at me. They'll be nothing left of me but a bag of tiddlywinks.

Okay, okay, I get it. I get it. I made up them regulations. I lied to you. You got me. What more do you want?

What? Oh, no. No, no, no, boy. You wait a minute now . . . you hold on there a cotton-pickin' minute . . . don't you even *think* about pointing that gun at yourself.

What the hell is wrong with you, boy? This ain't no suicide mission. You put that down right now.

That is a direct order, son! That is a command.

Please, boy . . .

Okay, look, son, I know you're scared: seventeen years old, war on TV every night; grunts covered in mud, babies crawling naked from burning huts, choppers and napalm and body bags and what all of that might mean for you someday, getting high to try and forget but not able to shake the thought that you'd be better off dead if killing someone was the only way to prove you were a man.

Well, I'm here to tell you, it's going to be okay, son. You know it's a game we've been playing at all these years. Right? We always came through every battle we ever fought. Didn't we? Got done fighting them Krauts and them Japs, washed up for dinner, said a few prayers and then went to bed, safe and sound. What's coming your way won't be any different than that, boy. You'll see. I promise.

You believe Joe, don't you, son?

Don't you?

That's it. That's it, son. That's right, put the gun back where you found it . . . Good boy.

Oh, now don't start crying. Come on, dry them eyes. Everything's gonna turn out alright. G.I. Joe is right here. Your old buddy Joe has got your back.

Look, kid, why don't you come on over here and pick up Joe off this shelf? What say you get some shut-eye? That's right, get on up and let's get over to that bed so you can catch some sack time. That's it, son. Grab Joe up under my little arms and carry me over there with you.

That's better, now, isn't it, boy? Us up here on this bed together— Joe keeping a look out? You rest, now, boy. You sleep it off. I'll call in our position.

Alpha Company reporting from the bed, sir! I got eyes on room. I got eyes on the door. All is clear. I repeat, all is clear. We're making camp here for the night.

All set, boy. All tucked in.

Man, listen to them crickets singing outside your window. You hear that? Remember how you used to believe that those chirps were angels singing, letting you know they were watching over you?

Good to be alive, isn't it? You and me here, me talking to you inside your head, making it all come out all right in the end. Just like we always did.

You know, boy, sometimes I think about us: you flesh and blood and me nothing but a lump of plastic. I mean, take off my uniform shirt, my pants and my boots and what's left—just string holding my pieces together, ball joints, injection-molded body. I don't even have a penis. But put us together and we make something real, don't we? Inside your mind here, together we make you a real little soldier. Everything your father ever wanted you to be, the reason you picked me up in the first place, whether you knew it or not, so you could become me and I could make you a man.

G.I. Joe. G.I. Joe. Fighting man from head to toe, on the land, on the sea, in the air . . .

God, I love that song. Sounds like America, don't you think, son?

You sleeping, boy . . . ? Well, that's okay. You sleep. You still got time before the real battle starts. Still time to dream you're the greatest *man* who ever lived in the greatest country that ever was. Tonight all is well. Tonight we'll fight and never die.

Incoming!

Enemy planes, hit the dirt!

All units commence firing!

Take the hill. Move out!

I promise, it's going to be the greatest fun you ever had.

AMERICAN FLYER

I'd been in the basement with Jack London trying to start a fire. The matches had dropped into the snow for a second time when my mother called me upstairs for dinner. All along as I'd been reading the story, the naked sixty-watt bulb above me had been swinging on its cord as someone or other moved around upstairs doing the real things that real people do. I didn't count myself among them. I didn't feel like any of the real people I knew. Not back then anyway.

Back then I lived with my parents and my sister in an old house in a dirty city in Connecticut. I attended an all-boys, Catholic high school where, already in my freshman year, I'd been voted most likely to be unlike anyone else. Back then, even the older brother I had who died at birth seemed to be more like the rest of my family than I was.

Getting off the old couch cushions I had dragged into the corner of the basement, I licked my thumb and forefinger and unscrewed the bulb above my head. In the dark I could smell my bad breath mingling with the mildew rising from the hundred-year-old pit I was standing in. Bits of mortar between the stones of the foundation came off gritty and damp on my fingers as I felt my way upstairs along the wall. I didn't mind any of this. I liked everything about being down there alone. Shuffling in my stocking feet on the packed dirt floor on my way to the stairs, I worked my way around the RCA cabinet radio, Formica-topped end table, bent lawn chairs, and a multitude of other household items that I had dragged down there, steadily building a living space for myself from the trash I'd found discarded on the street over the last couple of years on bulk pickup days.

At the table my father had already sat down. My younger sister, Tina, was next to him hanging her face over her place mat, her hair dangling around the rim of her dish.

"You know," my mother said to no one in particular. "Tomorrow will be eighteen years for Salvatore." She jangled her wristwatch and laid a platter of chicken parts on the table.

I did know. We all knew. Every year since 1952 my parents had noted the anniversary of my older brother's death at birth with solemn whispers, visits to the cemetery and masses bought with donations to the parish. Salvatore's death had been part of my life for as long as I could remember.

"Yeah," said my father, forking two chicken breasts out of the platter one after the other. "Eighteen years old. A man. Imagine that." My father looked at me, waiting for me to say something, as the muscles grew slack in his face.

I knew what was going on here. Though it had never been spoken, my stocky, balding father who I'd been named after was thinking about what it might have been like to have an older son who was not me, someone less flabby with more muscle tone and a package of character traits he could admire: honor and heroic strength, humor and self-control. These things would have come in handy in our house. Salvatore might have put them to good use diffusing the deep blue immigrant anxiety that filled our lives from the first cigarette my bony mother Betty lit rolling out of bed in the morning to my factory-working father's last check of the gas stove before we went to bed at night.

"Is there any more chicken?" I no longer wanted to talk about Salvatore. Besides, I was hungry and I'd only managed to get one piece off of the platter before my father took his and the rest were gone. I wanted to fill myself quickly and then get back to the fire that Jack London and I were trying to build.

"Why don't you finish the one on your plate first?" mumbled my father.

"One's enough for me," Tina murmured, picking a hair out of her mouth. I felt sorrier for her every time I saw her, breathing through her mouth, barely smiling, her breasts at twelve years old growing so quickly it frightened me.

"There's more in the pan." My mother started to stand up.

"He can get it." My father knifed into his chicken.

I changed the subject again.

"Bulk trash pickup tomorrow," I said.

"Huh?"

My father was jiggling his knee under the table. I could feel the floor quivering. I always felt somehow comforted when he did that.

"It's the bulk pickup day tomorrow," I said again.

His knee stopped shaking.

"Please don't bring home any more junk," he said.

I waited for his knee to move again, and when it did I got up and got another piece of chicken. I was thinking of what I might find in the trash tomorrow to add to my home in the basement. I also wanted to get back there to find out if we were going to live or die trying to make that fire.

The best piles of trash always seemed to be in front of the shittiest houses. At three p.m. the next day, right after school, I grabbed my wagon and headed over to a ratty side street I knew, about to see what I could find in front of some of the more run-down places that occupied the edge of our neighborhood. At fourteen years old, I was just reaching the full height of my adulthood; from a distance walking down that street I imagine I looked like a grown man pulling that dented American Flyer Wagon, pausing every so often to stoop and poke through the ruins at the curb.

Our town prided itself on its twice-yearly bulk trash pickup. Like most other cities, we had our two days a week where, rain or shine, we put out trash cans filled with our everyday garbage. But in early November and then again in late May, our city became more magnanimous and let its residents haul out larger objects that no longer had meaning in their lives.

Those lives, however, didn't include my life. I lived for those bulk trash pickup days. I never knew exactly what I was looking for. But when I spotted something I wanted, I became bold and nothing could stop me from towing it home. Along with the radio and chairs I'd found, I picked out and brought home everything from an art deco oscillating fan with a shaky steel cage, to an ornate vanity mirror, to an aluminum Christmas tree that had been molded into the shape of a *C* by the other much heavier items laid on top of it. One of these bulk pickup dives had netted me a cache of water-stained books, one of which was the book of Jack London stories I'd been reading. It was a book of short fiction filled with characters who matched what I wanted but was too afraid to be: a man who could escape on a whim, pursuing riches and glory and more life than was currently being offered to him.

That day, tugging my wagon around the corner of that side street, I spotted a small mountain of items in front of the second house on the left. This one-story house was a place so shabby and weather-beaten that it had taken on the look of a dust bowl farmhouse. The pile in front of it, however, held an array of tempting booty—metal objects that gleamed, old electronics, upholstery, porcelain and furniture only a little worn and dented.

The windows of this house were slatted yellowy-white with crooked venetian blinds. If anyone was home I could not see them in there. I pulled my wagon to a halt on the sidewalk about four feet from the pile. After pausing for a second, I took two steps in and looked over my shoulder up and down the street. Seeing no one anywhere, I bent into the junk pile and pulled on the rubber-capped handle of something I couldn't yet identify. When I could not free it, I tugged harder and when I did the red grip cap slipped off in my hand, catching me off balance. It also spooked me a bit, like I had pulled the leg or arm off of something living and small. Unstable and shaky in this way, I wasn't immediately sure if the voice I heard next was coming from inside or outside of my head.

"Hey." I jolted upright, the grip hanging from my fingers. "What d'you got in there?"

Whipping left forty-five degrees, I spun out of the pile toward a larger house next door that had been carved into first, second and third floor apartments. There, standing in the tall dead weeds of the front yard, was a boy of mixed and indeterminate race: Black, Hispanic, Asian, maybe a little dark Irish or Italian. It was hard to tell; his eyes were big and tawny and pinched at the corners, and his brown hair was curly, though I wouldn't have called it an Afro.

What stumped me more than his race, however, was the way he was dressed. He had on a man's button-down work shirt that fell to his knees over a pair of thin sweatpants, and he was barefoot despite the cold of November. He might have been seven or eight years old, but he was tall and skinny with long, dangling arms he didn't seem to know what to do with and a head too big for his body. Given the way he was dressed and how his parts seemed to be a little mismatched, he came across as something that had not yet been correctly assembled.

"That stuff don't belong to nobody," said the kid, "they left one night and the landlord piled it up."

"Oh." I nodded my head at the kid, thought about the situation for second, and then I nodded my head again before turning back into the clutter in front of the house. Despite any curiosity I had about him, this boy was not a threat to me, and if the house was vacant, so much the better.

I put the red grip back onto the handle and grabbed at metal this time, removing what turned out to be a toddler's scooter—a wood-and-metal mock-up of a World War II-era fighter plane with rubber wheels, stubby wings and handlebars poking out of the painted-on cockpit.

"That's mine," said the boy in the yard.

What was wrong with this kid? He was talking to me but staring up the driveway at a side door of the apartment house, his eyes darting between the door and a gold Oldsmobile that was parked at the bottom of the steps. The car was something out of the late 1950s with broken brake lights and mismatched tail fins.

"I thought you said this stuff didn't belong to anyone," I said.

"I wanted that," he said, pushing out his chin at the scooter in my hand.

"You're too big for it," I said.

"You are too."

He had me there. But if I hadn't wanted the scooter before, I was going to take it now on principle alone. I pulled it out all the way and put it in my wagon.

"You gonna sell that?" He looked at the side door and car and then back at me.

"No, I'm going to keep it."

"You gonna look stupid on that."

I was about to tell him to get away from me when both of us heard what started out like the growl of an animal before turning into the voice of a man bellowing from inside the apartment house.

"Bosco!"

The kid looked at me and I knew now why he'd been glancing at the car. The worry on his face was a 10X magnification of the expression he'd had when he was peeping up the driveway.

"You get your bony ass in this house, Bosco."

Hearing this disembodied command, the kid jumped and then spun toward the front door. He soared up the stairs of the house, disappearing into the gloomy brown of the front hallway, leaving the door open a crack behind him as he did.

Trying not to look too obvious, I leaned around the pile in front of the bungalow, squinting up into the hallway where the kid had vanished. And then I listened. I even held my breath so I could hear any faint sounds coming from inside the apartment house.

After a few seconds of this, I gave up and turned my attention back to the pile. I yanked out a suitcase-like portable phonograph with black musical notes printed on the lid, and a rusted bathroom scale.

I thought about digging further into the pile; there was a lot more decent stuff where the scooter, phonograph and scale came from. But my heart wasn't in it. My desire to return home with my treasures had leaked away. Whether it was momentary or not, I did not know. Though I have to say that it was still nagging at me as I picked up the handle of my wagon and went home.

When I rolled up our driveway a few minutes later, my parents and my sister were unloading gardening tools and empty plastic flowerpots from the trunk of my father's car. We did not have a garden. They had just come back from the cemetery.

"Where did you go?" my mother asked me.

My father looked at my wagon, fixating on the phonograph and its musical notations.

"Where did he go," said my father, neither needing nor especially wanting an answer. He slapped the flowerpots one inside another and shoved them at my sister who accepted them like an altar boy assisting a priest.

"I said a prayer from you for your brother," my mother said to me.

"I said one too," said Tina.

"That was an excellent prayer," said my father to Tina. "Salvatore would have liked it."

That my father thought he knew what a son who had never lived would have liked was a leftover of how crazy my parents had gone after their first child was delivered dead. From what I'd understood about it, they'd spent every cent they had on his funeral and then they agonized for days over his name—a fitting name for a dead boy who by some cockamamie tradition could not be named after his father—before they let him be buried. My grandmother Aida had whispered little secrets to me about my parents' grief at the time: how my mother wouldn't let the hospital take the baby for hours until they had to force her, screaming, to give him up; how my father had to drug my mother to sleep every night for a year before crying himself to sleep; how my parents would each talk to Salvatore when they thought they were alone in the kitchen or the backyard. By the time my parents got around to having me, their nerves were pretty much shot and, from what I've been told, the sight of a living baby who was not Salvatore did little to soothe their delicate conditions.

"I'm going to start supper," my mother said, flicking the dirt off a cheap pair or gardening gloves. "I thought I'd make a lasagna."

The way she said this, so brightly, I couldn't help but think that she was telling us she was preparing something special for Salvatore's birthday.

I had been waiting until they all went inside so I could safely move the junk from the wagon into the basement. But my father was not going to allow for the safe passage of these items without me passing through him first.

"Where are you going to put that?"

"Inside," I said, meekly.

"Where inside?"

"In the basement."

"Why do you have to bring home all this crap?"

"I'm fixing it up," I said, half-lying.

"For who?"

"For you or for mom maybe." I was *fully* lying now.

My mother, who'd stopped to listen when my father confronted me, leaned over the wagon and looked at the items in it.

"That's a nice thought," she said, her eyes dropping to make eye contact with me for a longer time that I felt comfortable having her do it. "Okay," she said, turning back to the doorway. "Why don't you put it all away now and get ready for dinner."

I cleared my throat.

"Do you want to come downstairs and see what else I've got?" I said this tentatively as my mother reached the doorway. I really wasn't entirely sure if I wanted them to come down there and look. But even if I wanted it, it turned out my parents did not.

"You heard your mother," said my father. "Put it away now."

He had totally ignored me. All these years later, I couldn't really tell you if I was thrilled or shocked to realize how frightened my parents were of seeing the life I was creating for myself down there under this other life they had built for me.

We died.

It turned out London hadn't gotten that fire going after all. Between having to go to school and my parents telling me to eat or sleep or do my homework, I had not managed to get back into the basement to finish the story until the day after I'd found the scooter and scale in the trash. When I finally did read the ending, I could not believe what Jack London had done. I was counting on him to keep us alive. Maybe we would have lost some toes or fingers to frostbite, maybe we would have been ashamed for being as stupid as we'd been to be out there alone with only a dumb husky to protect us. But why did we have to die? I hated him for doing that, and, finishing his story, I flung the book across the basement.

The book found its way past the array of junk I'd set up around me, until it hit a floor lamp I could never quite get to work, tipping it over onto a framed movie poster for *The Ghost of Frankenstein* that I'd nailed into the mortar of the wall, exploding the bulb at the top of the lamp and punching a web of cracks into the glass within the poster's frame. Now I was really pissed. I rolled off the mattress and when I got to the lamp I kicked it, bending the long, rigid leg it stood on. Having worn myself out causing this commotion, I stood there for a minute while things settled down. Objects stopped teetering. Glass finished tinkling. It was then that I heard a voice whispering from somewhere at the top of the stairs that lead to our back hallway and into the yard.

"Angie."

It was my father.

"What?" I whispered back.

"What's going on down there?"

"Nothing."

"Get up here." He was no longer whispering.

I hesitated, but seeing no choice, I climbed the stairs to stand face-to-face with my father silhouetted against the glass door that lead to our backyard. To my surprise, it had started snowing lightly outside while I'd been in the basement—an early snow in mid-November. I could see the thin flakes swirling on the other side of the louvered glass door.

"I'm getting tired of pulling you out that basement," my father said to me.

"I'm tired of you pulling me out," I said.

My father breathed harshly through his nose before shifting his weight onto one foot.

"It's time for you to get involved in other things."

"What other things?" I said.

"Things," said my father. "The things you have to do." He started jiggling his leg.

I knew exactly what he meant but fear has a way of making us stubborn.

"I like it down there."

"Yeah, well, I'm locking it up. I don't want you going down there anymore."

I knew he could do it and claim he was doing it out of love and for my own good by forcing me to face the world more fully. It would have been easy for him to padlock the slabs of oak that made up the doors to the basement, to lock me out for eternity.

"You can't," I said.

"I'm gonna," he said.

"You can't." I could feel the river rising in my throat, cresting behind my eyes.

"Yes, I can," he said.

"Well, fuck you," I said, beginning to cry. "And fuck everybody here."

I opened the back door and ran. It was cold in the yard, and I only had on the long-sleeve uniform shirt I wore to school tucked into a pair of brown polyester pants. I kept going anyway.

At the intersection of the driveway, I slipped on the leather soles of my shoes as they scuffed the snow that was sticking to the cold ground. Catching myself before I could fall, I began to jog on my tiptoes toward the street.

"Angie, get back in here."

Behind me in the doorway, my father had stalled. He was in his stocking feet and hesitant to follow me. This was good. Running now, I was not as cold.

"Angie . . . Angie for Christ's sake . . ."

On the sidewalk, I turned toward the northern territories of our neighborhood but before I passed our house, my sister stepped out onto the front porch.

"Where you going, Angie?" she said. The wind swept the hair off her face, surprising her and giving me the first glimpse I'd ever had of her beauty before another wind whipped it back again.

"Go back inside." I said, turning up the collar of my shirt.

"Don't . . ."

But ultimately I did, leaving her in front of the house where we had been born and lived.

The pile was still there in front of the bungalow. Those cowardly bastards in the sanitation department had left it there for another day, afraid of a little forecasted snow. Hugging myself, I slid to a stop about fifty feet from the mound, examining it from across the street. The edges and contours of the junk had been perked into life with the clean breath of winter newly born.

I had only come to look. The way a person looks at a monument. I didn't notice the movement within the pile until one of the edges of snow broke apart at the pile's center. The boy had been crawling around in there all the time I'd been looking at it.

"Get out of there," I yelled.

The boy stood up.

"Why I have to get out of here?" he said.

It was a good question, though what I really wanted to know was why he was out in the snow wearing the exact same outfit he was wearing yesterday? And where had the Oldsmobile gone? The spot it had occupied in the driveway was empty and there were tire tracks in the snow that trailed away from the house and down the street.

"It's mine," I said to the boy, pointing at the pile.

I knew the stuff didn't belong to me, but I didn't want this boy or anyone else in there mingling with what was left of it.

"It ain't yours," he yelled back.

I began to walk toward him, whereupon he frantically started pulling random items out of the pile, loading up his arms with a kitchen mixer, a girl's baby doll, Bakelite dishes and cups and as many other smallish things as he was able to get away with in a single haul. It was only when he got greedy and tried to pull out something larger—a ratty dog's bed, all frayed padding and chewed wicker— that everything fell from his arms onto the sidewalk.

"That's my stuff," he said, backing away as I approached. "Don't you touch it."

"Why are you out here in the snow?" I asked him.

"Why you?" he said.

"Does your father know you're out here?"

"He left."

"Well, what if he comes back?"

"What if he does?"

"He won't like seeing you out here digging through this stuff."

"He won't do nothing to me he ain't already."

"Don't you know you can die out here in the cold?"

He brayed like a donkey then, showing a fine set of white teeth and healthy, purple gums. He was about as far from death as you could get.

"I ain't cold at all. You cold?"

"Yeah," I said.

"Then go home." I moved closer.

We were maybe three feet apart now. This was the closest I'd been to him, and at this distance it took me by surprise to see that behind his too-big head and dangling arms was a real person getting ready to grow into them.

"I don't have a home," I told him.

"You're lying to me. You got a home."

"No, I don't," I said.

"Well, you better find one then."

I looked at the snow that had started to accumulate in the black ringlets of his hair. With this frosting added to the adult way he'd been speaking it wasn't hard to picture him morphing from a boy to a father to an old man. It was as if he'd gone off while I waited there, lived his life and was now back here once again, right where we'd started, the junk from the life he'd built piled up behind us at the curb. I bounced on the balls of my feet, wanting to do something but not knowing what. For his part, the boy seemed to be waiting, *wanting* me to do something.

"You know, I could make us a fire," I said.

"Yeah?" He seemed genuinely interested in this idea.

"Yeah."

"You got any matches?" he asked me.

"No," I said.

"Then how you gonna make us a fire?"

"I don't know," I said quickly, seeing the Oldsmobile turning onto the street behind us. I'd only had to catch a flash of the tail fins to know that it was coming our way in the snow. "We'll figure it out," I told the kid.

He nodded at me and smiled for the first time since I'd set eyes on him. This time, however, he didn't seem to notice the car, let alone care about it.

I looked over my shoulder. The Olds had stopped now. It was idling in the street about twenty feet away, the engine fuming. With the snow falling, I felt dreamy and oddly warm, and I swear to you that when I turned back to look at the boy, I could already see the flames beginning to rise.

EVERYDAY PEOPLE

The barefoot Black kid who's been pawing at my motorbike runs his eyes over my denim jacket and long hair.

"What the fuck you looking at?" I ask him.

The kid flinches and that's when I glance again at the girl sitting on her porch. She's beautiful—eyes green like sea glass, lips the shape of candy hearts, cocoa skin and a pillow of hair so big I could bury myself in it. Even still, I must be out of my mind trying to get her to look at me by picking a fight down here in this neighborhood.

"Ain't looking at nothing, brother," says the kid, touching the bike again.

"I'm not your brother. And get your hands off my bike."

He wouldn't even know how to ride it. And if he did, he wouldn't get far. Some cop would pull him over as soon as he turned the corner—barefoot Black kid on a barely used 1970, 125cc Kawasaki with no license plate.

"Alright, alright . . . *brother*," says the kid. "Ain't my fault you got such a nice motorcycle, I can't keep my hands off of it."

He is a wiseass, though. This kid. Getting tougher now, too, as a crowd of his friends close in.

"Yo, Santorelli, where's your boy Spendoli?"

This is Freddy Hughes, one of the Black kids we all kind of know from around here. He's stepping out of the crowd of soul brothers who've been watching, and he's pointing up the street, smirking. I stare at him like he's speaking a foreign language. But it is a good question. Where *is* Spendoli? I was supposed to meet him down here at the edge of this neighborhood to catch up with Bobo Ribisi and Johnny DeCarlo.

"I don't know, I ain't seen Spendoli," I say, spitting out the words.

"Well, you ain't seen him, you ain't seen him," says Freddy. "*Got* to believe that. Hard to miss that white face when it pops out around here."

"Why don't you go fuck yourself, Freddy?" I hear myself saying it and again I glance at the girl on the porch. This time her eyebrows are raised, and she's got a faint smile on her lips. She lowers her eyes, but I can tell that she likes to be looked at. Or maybe she just likes *me* looking at her.

"I don't need to fuck myself," says Freddy. "I got your momma doing that."

I start laughing like it's really funny. "Yeah, well my momma told me to give you this."

I jump on the Kawasaki, land on the kick-starter and twist the throttle until I have the bike headed right at Freddy's crotch. He pivots and then he starts hauling ass like a jackrabbit while the rest of his friends scatter.

I'm spinning donuts left and right trying to catch Freddy as he runs up and down Bishop Street, and I've almost got the front wheel of the bike up the slit of his ass, when he takes a sharp left and I punch the handle bars out as far to the right as they'll go. It's a smooth move that might have worked except that I've hit a patch of sand left over from the last storm of last winter. I wipe out and lay the bike down on the road at fifteen miles an hour.

Sliding to a stop, I can smell the denim burning off the exhaust pipe where the bike landed on my thigh. I twist back toward the frame of the bike and push at the gas tank. The girl must be watching me, so I make the bike seem heavier than it is to show off a little. Just as I lift it and I'm about to set it upright, I hear an evil-sounding voice, a kick-your-ass baritone, calling out from across a short distance away. It's *Luther*, of all people, and he's standing beside the girl on the porch. Luther: black beret, knee-length leather jacket, eighteen-year-old Black Panther about to take off his training wheels. Everybody knows about Luther. And now I'm wondering if that's his sister I've been staring at on the porch.

"Who told you could crash your motorcycle on my street, motherfucker?" says Luther.

Freddy and his crew, even the barefoot kid, are reassembling around me now, close enough for me to hear them mocking me and muttering. Up on the porch where Luther is standing, the girl is still watching me. The expression on her face is not disgust or satisfaction that I got what is coming to me. It's sympathy.

"What the fuck you looking at, Claris?" says Luther. "Get in the Goddamn house."

She turns to Luther, cocks her head and squints, dropping her right shoulder like a fighter setting up a punch. "Clar*eeece*," she says. "How many months do I have to live in this house before you learn how to say my name properly? My name is *Clarice*."

With that she turns back to me and begins to gaze hard from twenty-five feet away across the road—which feels like no distance at all and makes me feel like she and I might not be living in the same place as the rest of these people on the street, not even in the same year or on the same planet. It's not 1973, anymore, I'm not fifteen-almost-sixteen-years-old and this is not New Haven, Connecticut. It's no time and no place, and when she smiles at me this time I have to look away first, and now I'm feeling something else, something I never felt before and can't describe.

"Genie, you okay?"

Sure, *now* Spendoli shows up, running over from around the corner of Bishop and Lawrence. He could have been hiding back there watching the whole thing, chickenshit that he is. Even if he *is* trapped down here living in this not-so-white-anymore neighborhood.

"Yeah, I'm good," I say to Spendoli. "Let's get the fuck out of here."

The bike seems to be okay, scratched up but moving without any wobbles, and I'm rolling it away when Luther steps in front of me. Freddy and the other kids who've been milling around break apart.

"Don't come down here no more," Luther says. "Your boy can meet you up at *your* house from now on."

I can't tell if he's giving me friendly advice or some kind of secret warning.

"It's a free city," I say to Luther.

"Is for some of you'all," says Luther and I don't say anything else.

The muttering crowd of soul brothers becomes very quiet, the kind of quiet that makes you a little nervous. Though it doesn't seem to be bothering Clarice because she hasn't left the porch. In fact, she's sitting on the steps now, arms hugging her knees, watching me, not caring a bit what Luther is thinking as he stares at her.

I am home after hanging out with my friends for a couple of hours. Pushing my bike into the back of the garage where I'm hoping my father won't see the scratches, I find Douglas lying on the floor behind the snowblower, chewing on the head of one of my sister's Barbie dolls. The dog is almost six years old, old enough to be a middle-aged man, but I swear he's a little retarded. He sees me with the bike and he brings the doll's head over to drop it at my feet. I ignore him though he keeps picking up the head and dropping it in front of me until I get the bike into the garage behind the lawn furniture. This dog knows I'm a pushover and that on most days I'd take pity on him and toss around that doll's head for him to fetch.

I once asked my father why he named the dog Douglas, and this is what I got: "Kirk *Douglas*, toughest actor who ever lived, played a boxer and a gladiator and even made that faggot painter—what was his name, Van Gogh—even made *him* look like a real man." Sometimes I'm not sure who's more retarded, my father or the dog.

In any case, I'm glad to see that my father's municipal-owned Chevy Caprice is not in the driveway, only my mother's Buick Skylark tucked up in front of the lawn furniture and my bike. Brushing my fingers along the Skylark's fender, I wonder what might happen if I slipped into the house for the keys to run the car back down and see if Clarice is still there.

I can see myself *now*: I'm sitting inside the Skylark with Clarice. I've taken her on a joy ride, and we've parked the car in a spot at the base of East Rock where there are a lot of trees and not much else, and I'm kissing Clarice and she's kissing me back, and her left hand is resting on my crotch, and . . .

Douglas howls.

My father is pulling up the driveway in the Caprice, his partner Al DiNucci riding shotgun, looking like Frankenstein with a torso the size of a city mailbox, hands big as lawn rakes, and arms swinging like boat oars.

You gotta love these two together—Al and my father. Forget how mismatched they are in size. Their running nicknames for each other are enough to kill you. My father calls Al 'Spade' and Al calls my father 'Hammer'—Sam Spade and Mike Hammer. That's who they think they are—Sam Spade with bad hips and a bottle of Pepto-Bismol in the glove box of his unmarked police car, and Mike Hammer with arch supports, a bulging disc and delusions that anyone who's not the same color as him is out to do him harm.

I step to the front of the garage where my father could see me if he looked. Douglas, however, is way ahead of me. He's galloped all the way over to my father who's now so busy talking to him like he's a four-legged baby that he doesn't notice me standing there.

"Dougy, Dougy, Dougy . . . Did you miss me, killer?" My father is kneeling, rubbing Douglas's belly from his dick to his neck and back.

"Hey, Genie, wash the car, will you?" Having unpacked himself from the Caprice like the Jolly Green Giant let out of a can of beans, Al has spotted me standing inside the garage. "Vacuum the mats too," he says, as if he's invented comedy.

"Sure," I say. Can I keep the change I find in the seats?" I ask this in a way that might as well mean "fuck you," though Al is too dumb to hear that. My father, however, hears me and has picked up on my attitude. He's not fond of it.

"Where's your mother?"

"I don't know. Car's here." I point to the Skylark.

"Thanks, *Sherlock*. What the hell are you doing out here in the garage?"

Douglas, sensing my father is done with him, runs back over to me.

"Just putting the bike away," I say to my father.

"Where'd you go?"

"Riding around."

My father is rubbing the stubble on his chin and glancing toward the garage, up and over its roof as if he could get his eyes to cannonball down into Luther and Clarice's neighborhood.

"Yeah, well, make sure you stay up *here* with that bike," he says. "Or I'll take it away so fast your head will spin."

Douglas lies down at my feet—he loves everybody, this dog—and so to make Douglas happy and piss off my father I drop onto one knee, rubbing Douglas's belly exactly as my father did. I start to picture Clarice rubbing the dog's belly with me, and I feel myself get a little flushed and warm. Douglas likes Clarice. I like Clarice. Clarice likes me.

"Hey, you hear what I'm saying about staying out of that neighborhood?" my father shouts.

"Yeah, yeah, I hear you."

It is then that I decide I am going back to Clarice's house on my bike as soon as my father leaves to go back on shift with Al.

Three days go by and Spendoli, DeCarlo, Ribisi and me are squatting around the Kawasaki in front of Wozniak's drug store on the corner of Humphrey and State Street, when out of my right ear (my left being tuned into the bike which is idling on the sidewalk) I hear girls giggling. These are not white girl giggles. These are high-pitched, Baptist-church, don't-stop-me-now, Black-girl giggles. Cutting off the engine so I can tune in more closely, I realize one of the girls is Clarice.

I've ridden my bike on and off for three days around Clarice's neighborhood—hoping I'd see her sitting on her porch or walking to the store or hanging out at that scabby laundromat down there—not able to find her anywhere. But now, who would have guessed, she's decided to come strolling up here into *my* neighborhood.

Clarice and her two friends get closer, and I'm sure they're about to walk right past when she stops a few feet from me, turns to the girl on her right with six-inch platform Thom McAns, and speaks.

"Wait a minute, Ruby," says Clarice. "I've got to tie my shoe."

Five surprised faces look at Clarice's red, white and blue sneakers. I hesitate before glancing at Clarice's feet; she is close enough for me to smell her perfume, and I feel like I took a hit of dope that would have been too strong for somebody twice my size. It's only when I snap out of it that I notice Clarice is also not looking at her shoes. She's dropped to one knee—the ruffled edge of her short white skirt rising to show me the back of her thighs—and she's looking at *me*.

"Your shoe ain't untied, Clarice." It's the second girl with Clarice saying this. She's shaking her braided pigtails and eyeballing her friend with the platform shoes.

"The laces were getting loose." Clarice is pretending she's busy with her shoe but when she stands up again I'm ready.

"Where's your brother?" I ask.

I say it with an attitude that my friends will think is meant to mock Clarice and these girls, but that's far from the way I mean for Clarice to take it.

"Who?" she asks.

"Luther," I say, and Spendoli, DeCarlo and Ribisi start smirking.

"He's not my brother," says Clarice, and her two friends turn their heads from her to me and then back to her. "Luther's my mama's boyfriend's son," she says. "We're only living in their house until we can get a place of our own down here."

"Oh," I say. "Where you from?"

This is the kind of question to ask when you're in front of a girl you like. But there couldn't be a worse time or place for me to ask it. My three friends are looking at me now like I've lost my mind chatting up this girl, while Clarice's friends have gotten in front of her and are trying to block our view of each other.

"We came from Bridgeport," says Clarice, sidestepping her friend with the pigtails so she can get closer to me. "My daddy died and my mama met Luther's father at her job . . ."

"Come on, Clarice, we got to get downtown," says the girl with the platform Thom McAns.

"You want to get them tickets, don't you?" says the pigtailed friend.

"Yeah, alright. I'm coming." Clarice turns away. "I'm the one told y'all about that show in the first place," says Clarice, shrugging them off and walking ahead.

Clarice's friends scamper to catch up to her and just when I think I've lost her for good, she lets her friends walk past her and speaks again, loud and clear, to make sure I hear it.

"There's no way I'm going to miss Sly Stone at the Arena Tuesday night," she says. "No way I'm *not* going to be there." Cranking her head over her shoulder, she glances back to find me.

"Stop staring at the White boy, Clarice," the girl in the Thom McAn's hisses loud enough for us to hear.

But Clarice doesn't seem to care how much her friend hisses or what the eyes on this street aimed at us like sniper rifles will make of her and me. Instead, she drops her eyes down onto me, her lids covered in blue shadow closing over the two of us like a blanket before she's forced by her friends to turn and walk away.

I've counted down the days and plotted my strategy, and now it's Tuesday night and I've parked my bike at the edge of a surface lot across the street from the New Haven Arena. So now what? There are so many hundreds of kids banging around the front entrance, and so many girls who *could* be Clarice, that to find her I'm either going to have to be very lucky or very smart.

"Hey, kid, get that bike out of the way."

The surface lot attendant has caught me plugging his driveway, and he's not happy about it. Deciding to kill him with kindness, I very politely ask if he'd mind me parking my bike behind his booth for a minute. He thinks about that, looks past me and says, "You got any idea what can happen around here in a *minute?*"

Turning around, I see what he sees. White kids and Black kids mingling everywhere while all the cops brought on for extra duty stand tense as soldiers around the edges. It wasn't two years ago when a platoon of Italian and Irish policemen, along with a Crown Vic full of FBI lawyers almost started a riot when they put Al Seale and other

Black Panthers on trial two blocks away in the federal courthouse on Church Street. Right now in front of the Arena you've got White boys side by side with brown boys, blond girls bumming cigarettes from Black girls in African flag t-shirts, and all of them mingling and breaking into song—"Hot Fun in the Summertime," "Everybody Is a Star," "Family Affair." All I can think of is what my father would do if he saw what was going on in front of the Arena with me in a surface lot at the edge of it. Yes indeed, there is a lot that could happen here in a minute.

I roll the bike over to the back of the parking lot shack, drop the kick stand and wave at the attendant who is busy directing a car into one of the last open spaces.

"Okay, thanks," I yell at him, not waiting for a reply, after which I throw myself into the traffic: car horns honking, fists humping the air out of drivers' side windows.

On the Arena side of the street, an irritated Black man is shouting into the crowd. He stands a good six-and-a-half-feet tall, and weighs at least three hundred pounds.

"You got tickets, stand over *there*." He points to the middle door of the Arena. "You *want* tickets, stand over *there*." He points to the box office nearby. "You ain't got tickets and don't want tickets, get the hell out of here."

I look at the box office. *To find this girl I'm either going to have to be very lucky or very smart.* I study the middle door of the Arena where the kids who have tickets are supposed to be standing. Kids like Clarice.

The problem is I can't see well enough through this crowd to find out if Clarice is standing there. So I get up on my tiptoes. I start to crane my neck, but as I'm getting a bead on the situation, I hear a man bawling out my name from somewhere in the crowd behind me.

"Genie? Hey, Genie. Genie Santorelli."

At first, I'm curious, but then it hits me. I know that voice.

"Genie . . . Genie!"

It's Al DeNucci. Of course it is. The fucking oaf will do anything for overtime pay.

I drop down off my tiptoes to blend into the crowd. I need to avoid Al, and I'm hoping I can become invisible in the crush of people pushing and shoving me every which way—my elbows slamming into the spinal columns of overdeveloped Black boys, my rear end and groin grinding into kids who don't seem to know I'm there. I'm so overloaded by all this contact that at first it doesn't register when someone's soft, wiggling fingers tickle my wrist.

"Hey." This word is breath in my ear before the warmth of it turns into sound and then into more words. "You looking for somebody?"

My heart begins to rock like a drummer's paradiddle. I turn and I'm standing face-to-face with Clarice. A couple more inches and our lips would be touching.

"Yeah," I say, "I was looking for *you*."

We smile at each other and it goes on long enough for Al DeNucci to spot me again. He jacks his bulk into the crowd to get closer.

"Can we go somewhere else?" I ask, leaning into Clarice's ear.

"I've got a ticket," she says, protesting, though I'm pretty sure her attitude is more for show and just for now.

Before I can be certain, however, somebody inside the Arena fires up a recording of another one of Sly Stone's hits. They've played this one in particular to whet the appetite of the crowd and it's working. Music and lyrics come blaring out through bullhorn speakers over the entrance doors, and the crowd loosens up considerably as they start to boogie and jump and sing.

Sometimes I'm right and sometimes I'm wrong . . . my own beliefs are in my songs . . .

"We'll come back. I promise." I shout this at Clarice and, before she can think about it, I grasp her arm, moving us toward the curb and freedom.

The butcher, the banker, the drummer and then . . . Makes no difference what group I'm in . . . I am everyday people . . .

"Hey! Kid. Hold up." Back there somewhere Al is yelling. His voice no longer his *Genie-why-don't-you-wash-the-car* voice. His voice now just that of an angry White cop.

Clarice and I run. At the street, I put my arm around her waist to guide her through traffic. In return she rests her hand in the small of my back; and a shiver goes through me. This tight together we have to slow to a waddle to cross the street, but we finally get to the other side, stopping not far from where I've parked my Kawasaki.

I know I am going to kiss Clarice and that she is going to kiss me back. Neither of us could stop this from happening if we wanted to. Unfortunately this is also when Luther decides to show up.

I have no idea how he knew to end up here. Maybe he's been watching Clarice all along. Whatever it was, there he is, swaggering toward us on the far side of the surface lot. Worse than that, a step behind Luther on either side of him are two other Black men a good decade older than Luther, both of them wearing goatees and angry expressions.

Am I going to let Luther and his friends stop me from kissing Clarice? You bet I am. Though Clarice is not going to let them stop *her*. She leans in and kisses me on the mouth before pulling away.

"What the fuck you doing, Clarice?" Luther is shouting as his two friends hold him back.

Clarice tilts her head away from me to taunt Luther with a smile.

"Get your ass over here," Luther yells.

"Easy, man," says the guy to Luther's right.

"Let it be," says the one on the left. "This ain't no thing for you right now."

Hearing this, I get a little braver.

"Come on?" Clarice hesitates as I make it clear what I have in mind. "Get on the bike."

I sweep my arm out to the left, pointing to my motorcycle a few feet away behind the booth. For a second it looks like Clarice won't move, but before I know it, she is on the back of the bike and I've taken a running leap onto the seat. She puts her arms around my ribs, and I choke the carburetor and kick. Hard. Lifting my head from the handlebars, I can see that Al has finally bullied his way through the crowd. The only thing keeping him from lurching across Crown Street is the green light allowing the traffic to speed by in front of him.

Al is shouting something and, though I can't hear what it is over the engine noise and music blaring from the Arena's bullhorns, I can guess. "Goddamn it, kid," he's saying. "Don't do this. You ain't gonna like what happens if you do this."

He would be right, of course, if that's what he was shouting. I'm *not* gonna like what happens if I do this: not gonna like what happens with my father; not gonna like what happens in my neighborhood with my friends or in the world that revolves around Luther and his friends; not going to like any of it up and up all throughout America from there.

But now is not the time to think about what might happen in the future. Now is the time to think about how Luther has broken free of his friends, and how Al has gotten the red light and is running faster than I ever thought a man that big could run.

"Where are we going?" asks Clarice, her voice vibrating as I rev the bike.

"Away," I yell.

I twist the throttle and the bike leaps from behind the attendant's booth, rearing up into a wheelie on the sidewalk before we land on Crown Street. In front of us is a police car parked in the fire lane we're using to make our escape. Squeezing past the car, I weave into traffic, cutting across the lane that runs by the Arena.

Accelerating now, I can see Al DeNucci in my rearview mirror trailing us on foot. He's too far away to catch us, but he has begun whistling and shouting to get my attention and the noise he's making has piqued the interest of some of the kids on the sidewalk in front of the Arena. A small army of boys, their mouths open in laughter, reorganize themselves in the street to try and stop Clarice and me, but before I have to hit the brakes to stop us from hitting *them*, Clarice raises her fist in the air and starts swinging. One by one the boys back away to give us room to drive past. I've never seen anything like it in my life—a single girl with the power to hold off an army.

I gun the throttle and swerve back into the center lane, squeaking left to ride in a tight line between a yellow cab and a Toyota Corolla. Running full-out away from the Arena, I can still hear the music from under the marquee.

We got to live together . . .

Clarice shifts her position on the back of the bike, her hands snugged into the side pockets of my jacket.

"I'll bring you back later when things quiet down," I shout over my shoulder.

"I don't want to come back," says Clarice.

"What about the concert?" I yell.

Clarice doesn't answer me. All I have to do to understand why is to take another peek in my rearview mirror.

I can see Al DeNucci standing alongside Luther and his two friends, the four of them watching us roll away. From this distance, you'd almost think they all found something to unite in—the way they're standing there quietly side by side, dumbfounded. You'd almost think that, wouldn't you? Though Clarice might tell you differently.

Still, watching Al and Luther get smaller in the distance, I'm wondering if I should be as afraid of them as I've been. It's not because we've gotten away together, Clarice and me. It's because, somewhere in my gut it's hit me that there's really *nothing* they can do to us. Sure they'll try to make our lives difficult now, but what then. The future, that *horrible* future that guys like Al and my father want me to think is coming, that future has got to be a lie. Guys like Al and my old man can never really stop anybody from loving anybody they want. Al will die someday. My father will die. Even the Panthers will all someday die. And when that happens, everyday people like Clarice and me and a billion others like us, we'll win. I'd like to believe that anyway.

"You ain't supposed to be riding this motorcycle down here, are you?" Clarice asks loudly into the hair trailing down my neck.

"No," I yell over my shoulder. "I'm not supposed to be doing any of this."

Seeing an escape route ahead, I break free of the jam on Crown Street to maneuver down a narrow block that leads into a quieter section of downtown. Shivering on the seat behind me, Clarice puts her chin on my shoulder.

"It's okay," she says. "Let's keep going."

I lean back until her nose is touching my cheek.

"You like dogs?" I ask.

"I do if they like *me*," she says.

"He'll like you," I call back to her.

"Who?"

"Douglas," I say, slowing the bike so that the engine is no longer screaming.

"That's a funny name for a dog." Clarice giggles.

"I didn't name him," I say, "it wasn't *my* idea."

But Clarice already knows that. I can tell by the way she's resting her cheek on my shoulder that we're in this together now. That everything we know we'll know together, and for a long time to come.

DEUS EX MACHINA

Dear God.

Standing at the bathroom sink, a marble font he'd imported from Italy, Carlo held the blade from his safety razor between his thumb and forefinger, staring at himself in the mirror.

I'm not asking for much here.

Carlo had been thinking about God this morning. How God might help him with the trouble he'd found himself in.

I've given so much and I've asked for so little in return.

Honestly, why shouldn't he expect God to be there for him now? He was, after all, a lifelong Catholic, steeped in the cold broth of God's edicts via a harsh cluster of nuns at various Catholic schools, unquestioningly carrying that burden year after year through every sacrament and holy day, delivering first himself, and then his wife plus four children, to church each and every Sunday, a standing appointment on his calendar.

I need your help, God. And, really . . . I mean . . . you'd have to agree I've earned it. We both know how far I've risen from where I began.

God may have made Carlo, but it was Carlo who had made himself rich, rarely asking God to intercede with any special assistance, only that He adore him as a creature made in *His* likeness. All the more so for what Carlo saw as his *astounding* success in rising from poverty and ignorance to leave behind the immigrant ugliness of his family—his father's brutality, his mother's superstitions, his brothers' vulgarity, crookedness and incompetence.

Could you call what I've done this time a sin? I don't think so. A mistake, perhaps. Perhaps a large, technically unlawful mistake, but really nothing more than an error in judgment, given that I had every intention of making good on what I'd borrowed.

Then again, if Carlo truly wanted God's help, maybe he needed to formalize it in some way. An actual prayer might be in order. Perhaps an Act of Contrition.

God, I am sorry for my sins with all my heart. In choosing to do wrong and failing to do good, I have sinned against you . . .

But that wasn't right either, because, more than not believing he'd sinned, Carlo didn't think he'd done wrong. Not really. All he'd done was try to save his business by injecting cash into it during the worst real estate market he had ever faced. Though his partners and the banks weren't likely to see it that way once they got to the bottom of it. Plus this time the police were getting themselves involved.

In truth, all Carlo really wanted from God was to create a little more time for him, enough time for Carlo to find the money and pay back the loan he'd taken against the office complex he managed. Perhaps God could have the fraud detective that left his card at Carlo's offices get into a nonfatal car wreck, putting him in the hospital for a week or two. Or better than that . . .

Dear God, we in America, at this time—1980, the year of your Son our Lord—are facing a crisis of seventeen and one-half percent mortgage interest rates. If you could see it in your Sacred Heart to convince the Federal Reserve to lower these interest rates and bring back the housing market, so that I might once again run my business in the black.

Carlo looked at the razor blade in his hand. He'd taken out a fresh blade in order to shave.

I've gotten myself out of these things before and with your help, God, I'll do it again.

In the mid-seventies he had 'loaned' himself money from some of his buyers' escrow accounts and, just when he thought he'd never be able to pay it back—was sure he was going to end up in jail—he'd made a killing on a block of apartment buildings. Three years ago there was that thing with the fire in the housing development he'd underwritten where you could argue that he'd not done things strictly up to code. Somehow he'd gotten out of that too.

He closed his eyes and with his free hand, Carlo rubbed the spot above the bridge of his nose, the place where Milton, that idiotic, crystal-wearing fiancé of his oldest daughter, told him was where the Hindus believed we had a third eye.

Help me with this problem, God. Please. You helped me figure it out before and you can help me figure it out again.

Carlo looked down at the razor blade glinting. Something jumped in his chest. His throat tightened and the room started to spin. The light from the blade twirled against Carlo's eyes in direct proportion to the gyration of the walls around him. He flung the razor into the sink and gripped the ornate faucet above the basin to stop himself from falling to the floor.

What is happening to me, God? Help me, please.

His legs going weak under him, his heart thrashing against his ribs, Carlo hugged the pedestal of the sink, sliding down until he was lying on the granite of the bathroom floor.

Is this the end for me, God? Tell me, I beg you.

Carlo looked up toward the ceiling of the bathroom where he'd had an artist paint a mural of clouds and winged angels to go along with the Venetian theme he'd wanted in this house on a hill. The house he'd fantasized about having ever since he was a boy.

What should I do? Where do I go from here?

An hour later, Carlo had driven himself to the doctor's office. Dr. Mancini was an old friend of the family and Carlo had a great deal of respect for him. That rare Italian American who Carlo believed had been educated to his standards. Dr. Mancini was not a 'primitive' Italian like the members of Carlo's family: one of those deeply flawed men who wore callousness and incivility like a badge of honor decades after they arrived in this country. Dr. Mancini was a civilized man and because of this, because of his scientific mind, Carlo trusted him.

"I don't like what I see when I look in your eyes, Carlo," said Dr. Mancini.

Carlo nodded expectantly. He was sitting on an examination table, his wrists poking through the sleeves of a Johnny coat that he'd left untied at the back, cold air from a ceiling vent flowing down the ridges of his spine.

"What do you see?" asked Carlo, trying to control his breathing. "What's happening?"

All his adult life, Carlo had been meticulous about having precise and systematic medical attention paid to his body. He kept a separate file drawer in his office at home that held the results of every medical test and examination he'd had for the last twenty-five years, reports he could grab whenever he went to visit a doctor to have yet another test or examination. He'd brought the file with him today. He had it right on the chair where he'd draped his suit coat and pants.

"All my recent examinations have been normal," Carlo said, gesturing at the file. "Although something wasn't right this morning."

"You said." Dr. Mancini switched off the light in the scope he'd been using to look into Carlo's eyes. "You're telling me that you got dizzy and there was pressure behind your eyes?"

"Yes. My heart felt irregular, as well."

Go ahead, God, have him tell me that it is a small benign tumor, the beginnings of a heart condition, a rare but manageable disease . . . I can take it.

"Perhaps there was something we missed during one of my visits," said Carlo. He motioned to the file again in case Mancini had missed it the first time. "I brought my file with all the test results."

"I already have copies of all your tests," said Dr. Mancini. "I looked them over before I walked in here. Your body's healthy. Healthier than mine, I'd say. In fact, I'd like to put your chart up on that wall over there so I could point to it when my other patients come in—give them something to shoot for."

Tell him there is something wrong with me, God. Tell him the world takes pity on a sickly man, no matter what he's done to deserve otherwise.

"Have you been under an unusual amount of stress lately?"

"I thought you said that you didn't like what you saw when you looked at my eyes."

"Yes, well . . . your pupil dilation is sluggish, but that could be the residue of some anxiety, a response to fear . . . a holdover maybe from some sort of panic attack."

"I don't believe that was it," said Carlo. "I had some very precise physical symptoms."

Carlo took a breath and closed his eyes. Since God didn't seem to be helping out here, he was trying to find some thought that might calm him. All that came to him, however, was the memory of an affair he'd had about a year ago with a divorced woman whose house his agency had been trying to sell. He could hear her screaming as she had an orgasm and saw himself placing his hand over her mouth to quiet her down. He'd felt as out of control in that situation as he did right now with Dr. Mancini.

Carlo snapped open his eyes to find that the doctor had been watching him intently.

"I'm sure what you experienced felt very much like something physical," said Dr. Mancini.

"Yes, that's right."

"Well, as I said . . . " Dr. Mancini let his body drop onto an examining stool, rolling himself closer to the table then waiting until he had Carlo's full attention. "Look, Carlo, is there something going on that you want to talk about?"

"There's nothing to talk about," said Carlo.

Dr. Mancini nodded.

"Okay, Carlo," said Dr. Mancini. "I'll have to take your word for it, won't I?"

Why did you lead me here, God, if he isn't going to help me? I had respect for him. I put him on a pedestal.

The air from the vent above Carlo rustled the back of his Johnny coat, startling him with its timing.

"You can get dressed now," said Dr. Mancini.

"That's it?" said Carlo.

"No. I'm going to write you a prescription for Valium. It'll take the edge off whatever you're going through."

"What I felt was real."

"I'm sure whatever you're going through is very real."

Carlo went to the pharmacy and had the bottle of Valium tucked into his inside suit-coat pocket by the time he got to his office. Parking his car outside the over mortgaged building he owned, he took note of the people using their lunch hours to get to the bank or pick up food or fill their cars with gas. Stewing over this, Carlo began to despise these hordes for the money they were bringing into the businesses all around him. His own business was excruciatingly slow; no one was buying houses or any sort of real estate, unless it was a foreclosure. Somehow, these people on the streets were complicit in all of it.

Stepping off the sidewalk where he'd been standing, Carlo walked into his office. The receptionist looked up.

"Oh, Mr. Santorelli. "

She started rustling through the buck slips of telephone messages on the solid cherry reception desk that Carlo had built for this flagship office of his small-town empire: *Santorelli & Celestini Real Estate*, though there was no longer any Celestini, Carlo having bought out and buried the old man some ten years ago now.

"You've had a number of calls," said the receptionist.

Carlo looked at her suspiciously. "Who called?"

She handed him a disorganized stack of pink and yellow notes that had been ripped off a message pad. Carlo glanced through them.

"These are not organized in order of when the calls were taken."

"I'm sorry, Mr. Santorelli."

Carlo caught sight of himself in the glass that covered a zoning map on the wall behind the reception desk. He was stooped, hunched over. This was the last thing he wanted to let people see right now, a man who appeared to be hiding a secret. He threw back his shoulders and squared his face at the receptionist.

"Don't let anyone disturb me. If anyone comes in, tell them I'm not here."

The receptionist nodded and Carlo could see that she was afraid to speak to him. Good. So much the better. Right now he needed to get into his office and open the safe.

His backbone rigid, Carlo walked toward the back of the reception area and into his office. Wasting no time, he made his way over to a bookcase. Kneeling in front of it, he knocked some books to the floor and sprung open a panel that exposed the safe he'd instructed the builders to put there. He spun the dial and when the lock clicked, the safe swung open exposing the cash that remained inside. The exact amount between him and his ruin.

He counted it once, and then he made himself count it a second and third time until it finally sunk in that there was a *lot* less than he remembered.

Dear God, where did it all go?

This was where he had stashed the loan money after he'd cashed the bank check, but for weeks now he'd been using it to pay off other bills, other loans—the mortgages on his house and office building, the credit card notices from his wife's and kids' endless spending, the notes on his three cars, et cetera—all of it to keep his life afloat. His goal in coming into the office was to check on what was left of the money he'd taken to see if there wasn't enough of it left to make an honest effort in coming forward, admitting what he'd done and giving back what was left as a gesture of good faith to his partners.

Now, holding less than ten thousand dollars of the hundred thousand he'd taken, Carlo realized that this was folly. He'd paid bills so fast with this money that all he would be doing now by giving back what was left of it, was showing what a rapacious and reprehensible character he really was.

Dear God, what do you want me to do?

He was so deep inside his head, that when the buzzer went off on the desk behind him, it scared the prayers right out of him.

"Mr. Santorelli." Carlo froze at the sound of the receptionist's voice coming through the speaker box on his desk. "Mr. Santorelli . . . ?"

He slid himself away from the safe, across the floor on his knees until he was in front of the massive antique banker's desk of which he had always been so proud.

"What," said Carlo, his nose peeking over the top of the desk, his hand reaching across the blotter to hold down the *talk* button on the intercom.

"There was a detective here to see you." Carlo stopped breathing. "He left his card for you yesterday, but I told him you weren't here and to come back later."

Carlo dropped to the floor and slid himself under the desk, head bent, arms around his knees.

"Mr. Santorelli?"

Hail Mary, full of grace, the Lord is with thee.

Carlo kept up this prayer until it was displaced by a more compelling thought.

The Valium.

The pills were in his pocket.

Pulling the pill bottle out of his suit coat, he held it out to read the label.

"Take one pill as needed, one to two times daily."

He shook out three of the pills and put them in his mouth, waiting a few seconds until he'd made himself believe that he could feel the first flickers of his mind going numb.

Carlo looked up at the underside of the desk. *What now, God?*

The intercom screeched above him and Carlo flinched, hitting his head.

"Goddamn it!"

"Mr. Santorelli . . . are you in there? What are you doing?"

By five p.m., standing across from the table in his dining room, Carlo felt like he was flying. He'd snuck past the receptionist when she'd gotten up to go to the bathroom, and then he'd driven around town for hours, past a number of the houses his agency had listed but could not sell: Tudors and ranches, colonials and custom-builds, all on the market for nine, twelve and, in some cases, eighteen months. Even with the three valium he'd taken, each house he drove past gave him a twinge more anxiety, and when those twinges added up to more than he could handle he'd popped another pill. He was up to five or six by the time he'd gotten home for dinner with his wife, Angela, his youngest daughter, Sophia, and his oldest daughter, Isabella, who had also brought along her fiancé, Milton. His two middle children—a third daughter, Allegra, and his only son, Charlie, both in their early twenties—had left his house quite abruptly to live on their own in meager accommodations when they were barely out of their teens. It was a rejection he'd never quite understood given the luxuries he'd provided for them.

That Carlo was here was not so much because he felt a strong paternal duty to be home in time for dinner. It was that the more he'd driven around looking at his listings, and the more doped up he became, the more certain he was that God wanted him to go home to be with his family, those people who he believed loved him most and might somehow help him out of his jam.

The problem was that these people in the dining room did not quite seem to be the people he remembered. Standing in the doorway, gripping the molding to keep himself steady against the effects of the Valium, he recognized the faces, but their actions looked strange, the actions of people he didn't know.

"Why are you standing like that, Daddy?" Sophia asked.

"Where?" Carlo said, unnerved.

"There, in that doorway," said his wife, sitting down. "What are you looking at?"

"I'm admiring all of you," said Carlo.

"You look like you're high," said Isabella.

"I am not *high* . . . or whatever you call it . . . young lady." Carlo pushed himself hard to organize his head. "Can't a man let himself stand here and feel the love of his family?"

His daughters began to laugh while Milton looked on silently.

"Stop it, both of you," said Carlo's wife. "And you, Carlo, sit down, please?"

Carlo hesitated.

"Do you need a hand, Mr. Santorelli?" asked Milton. The boy was nothing but innocent kindness. Carlo sensed it, though there was something about Milton that annoyed him.

"I do not," said Carlo, pushing off from the doorjamb. It was such an endeavor to move to the table in a straight line that he was happy to have it over with once he got there.

"So, what happened today, Carlo?" his wife asked.

"Happened?"

What does she know, God? Have the police been here too?

Angela furrowed her brow.

"Yes. How was your day?"

"I'm glad you brought that up."

Carlo reached for a water glass. He'd wanted to take a sip to ready his voice for a monologue about mistakes and how we all make them. But as he brought the glass to his lips, he misjudged the position of his mouth and the water dribbled down his chin and onto his shirt.

"My God, Carlo," said Angela. "What is wrong with you today?"

Carlo fumbled to find a napkin to wipe his face and shirt. When he couldn't quickly lay his hands on one, Milton handed him his own napkin.

"Here, Mr. Santorelli. There's some water on the table too."

Milton watched as Carlo looked for the wet spot.

"Right here." Milton took the napkin back and dabbed the water on the table. He then lifted the napkin and pressed it into the damp area on Carlo's chest.

Carlo snagged the napkin from Milton and wiped his face. Milton looked away but the boy's empathy did not escape Carlo's eye. Milton was soft spoken. Milton wore simple clothing. Milton did not adorn himself except for that one crystal stone that hung round his neck on a leather cord. He was so unlike the all-consuming, double-loud family Carlo had raised in this opulent house. How did his brassy, outspoken daughter, Isabella, ever end up with this quiet, philosophical boy?

"Did Mommy tell you about the banquet halls we looked at today for Isabella's wedding?" said Sophia. Angela looked at her daughter crossly and slowly turned to Carlo.

"I was going to tell you after dinner. I'm still negotiating the prices."

"Milton and I don't really want it to be huge," said Isabella. Milton nodded agreeably. "We're going to cap it at two hundred and fifty people, max."

Carlo began to fidget in his chair.

Please, God, make this stop. Give me the strength to tell them we can't do this, that there's no money left to do this.

"We don't need to have that many people, Mr. Santorelli," said Milton. "If it were up to me, we'd have the wedding in a park."

"There's no fucking way I'm having my wedding in a park," said Isabella to Milton.

Okay, God, I give up. I can't stop this madness. I'm too weak. Help me, please.

"It's okay, Mr. Santorelli," said Milton, chuckling. "I'll keep working on her." The boy smiled sweetly.

Studying Milton's face, Carlo was suddenly shocked by the sight of a third eye peering at him from the lower part of Milton's forehead. It had to be the Valium, of course; Carlo's eyes were crossing in and out and that was probably creating the illusion. Still, Carlo saw it as a sign, believing that Milton might have insights that he had not yet admitted. Could it be that Milton was the one God had been telling him to seek out to save him?

Oh, dear Milton, please keep talking to them. They'll listen to you, Milton. They will. God has put you here to help me with my family.

"Shut up, Milton," said Isabella. "We agreed we're having a *real* wedding."

Milton's face sagged and all he could do given the blowback of Isabella's broadside was to nod and shrug and lean away from Carlo. Milton had become the face of the spiritual world for Carlo, and now that face had turned away because of his family's greed and aggression. A family Carlo had made in his own likeness.

I see what I've done, God. I've corrupted everyone, and now they're forsaking me as I've forsaken them.

At that moment, Carlo knew with certainty where God had been pointing him.

"I have a phone call I have to make." He stood abruptly.

His wife and daughters looked at each other.

Ignoring them, Carlo wobbled away from the table until he got to the doorway of the dining room where he turned around for one last look. There were his wife and daughters staring at him. And there was Milton, sitting quietly, gazing down at his folded hands, as if shrouding himself in prayer.

When he got to the bar less than an hour later, Carlo could not believe how dark it was. Likewise, how empty of patrons, or nearly thus. Besides the gone-to-seed female bartender, there was but one other customer, someone who appeared to be sleeping with his head down on a table near the front door, his back a hump of fat, his thick arms fused with the tabletop. The lighting in the bar had been boiled down to the red and blue-black afterburn of two neon signs—one hanging in the front window claiming the place as *The Three Jokers*, and the other pitched over the bar advertising *Dewars, It Never Varies*. This lighting, along with the seedy bartender and the monstrous man at the table, put Carlo in mind of a torchlit, medieval chamber.

"You . . . !" The man with his head on the table popped up and pointed at Carlo.

"Excuse me . . . I'm looking for . . ." Carlo backpedaled toward the door.

"It's okay." A dark-haired man in an open-collared shirt stepped out of the shadows at the back of the bar. "He's looking for me," he said to the bruiser.

"Eddy," said Carlo. "I wasn't sure if . . . "

"Yeah," said Eddy. "Sit down."

Carlo moved to sit at a table about midpoint between the bar and the door.

"No," said Eddy. "Over there."

He gestured to an empty café table in a corner of the room. Carlo got up, moved to the new table and sat down across from his brother Eddy who had already claimed a seat facing the front door. Carlo could not see much of Eddy's face from where he sat. Then Eddy leaned in closer and his features began to emerge: the cliff face of his nose and the craggy hillocks of his cheekbones appearing in a Martian dawn of red neon light.

"So, brother . . . you want a drink?" asked Eddy.

"No, no, we should get to it. I have . . ."

"Yeah, let's get to it, we really should."

Eddy lifted his hand toward the woman who was tending bar and she skipped over to him with a drink.

"You look like shit, Carlo," said Eddy, sipping from the rim of the glass.

"As I told you on the phone, I'm in a situation." Carlo watched Eddy sip again.

"And what situation would that be, brother?"

"Simply put, I need money." Eddy put down his glass loudly. "Of course, I would pay you back." Eddy stared at Carlo and then he let his eyes roll down to where Carlo's right hand was tapping against the top of the table. "With interest, of course," said Carlo.

"Interest," Eddy said, and Carlo nodded.

Reaching across the table, Eddy touched Carlo's wrist, sending what felt like a trickle of tiny worms into the veins of his arm.

"You know, brother," Eddy said. "When you called and told me you'd found yourself in a situation, I was wondering what that situation might be."

Playing his part, Carlo put on that practiced face of his. The one that said, "I am interested in what you have to say. I will turn myself inside out and become whatever you need me to be if you give me what I want." It was a face he had perfected in boardrooms and bank offices. And yet as soon as he put on this face he could see that this was not the place for it. His brother was a man who also had faces he wore, and the face that Eddy was showing Carlo was the face of a man who was willing to see his older brother suffer.

"What could this *situation* be, I thought," said Eddy. "Could this be a situation like the time when Carlo cheated his partner out of his share of the business he'd built, that poor, old sick man who was about to die."

"That was not what happened," said Carlo.

"Or is this more like that situation when my big brother was fucking that pathetic, divorced nymphomaniac in the bedroom of the house he was trying to sell for her, after so many years of being a self-righteous prick about the women the rest of us fucked."

"How do you know about that?"

"Or maybe, I thought, maybe this is a situation like when our parents wanted money to buy a place of their own so they could get out of that two-bedroom outhouse they rented, and Carlo refused to help them, even though he was the one with the connections and the cash back then, and even though it meant they'd go on living in that shithole for the rest of their lives if he didn't." Eddy drilled his gaze into Carlo's face.

"You have completely misconstrued what happened."

"Because this couldn't be a situation, I thought to myself, where my big-spending, civic-pride-parading, arrogant asshole of a brother broke the law and took money out of property that didn't belong to him. This couldn't be a situation like that, could it?"

"You listen to me now, Edward. I'm not going to beg."

"No, no, no. You don't have to beg." Eddy smiled calmly. "I won't make you beg."

"Well then. As I said, I need to borrow some money."

"Money's easy, Carlo. I can give you money."

"Alright then."

"But I'm not going to give you any money, Carlo. I'm not going to give you a fucking dime. Because that's not what you need. Money's got nothing to do with what you need," said Eddy. "What you need, Carlo, is to go away now—to go far away from here. *Far away*."

The bar sign in the window flickered, the word *Three* between the words *The* and *Jokers* buzzed before the red neon gas relit itself. To Carlo it looked like an omen.

"I don't like what you're suggesting," said Carlo.

"I'm not suggesting anything. Just that you go away. How you do that is up to you."

"And why would I do *that*?"

"Because, Carlo, you're not man enough to stay here and face what you've done. You never have been and now you've got no choice but to go away or go to jail. How's *that* feel?"

So that's it, isn't it, God? I understand what you want. I do.

Eddy reached into his pocket and pulled out a neat roll of cash.

"What's that?" Carlo asked.

"I changed my mind," said Eddy.

Carlo leaned a smidge closer and Eddy tossed a couple of bills over the table.

"Here's a hundred bucks," said Eddy. "Put a down payment on a funeral for yourself."

Arriving at the doors of Saint Aedan's, Carlo found himself caught in the beam of a midnight moon that had risen between the twin spires of the church. He'd been circling the streets since he left the bar, getting a little closer to the church at each turn, trying to build up his courage. Now that he was here, however, standing on the sidewalk tilting up at the church's bell towers, he felt very little in the way of courage.

Reaching into the vest pocket of his suit coat, Carlo took out the Valium. He spilled what was left of the pills into his palm. Placing his hand into the side pocket of his suit coat, Carlo took out a pint bottle of brandy he'd bought in a liquor store he'd passed by on his drive.

He put the pills in his mouth, uncapped the brandy, and drank until the pint was gone. Then he stumbled up the steps of the church to pull the handle of the door.

Carlo had been fixated on what he'd do when he got into the church—striding down the aisle, tiptoeing up the steps of the altar, quietly laying himself down under the apse. He'd never once thought that the door to the church might be locked. It had to be a mistake; God's house was never shut to those in need. But when Carlo tried the door again, it didn't open. Not a wiggle.

Carlo began to knock on the door, at first more or less politely. But as the liquor and pills began to take effect, he started to bang harder. Soon that turned into something more desperate, more like a wild animal ramming a cage, and Carlo began beating his fists on the door and howling like a fiend.

You will not let me die on the streets like an animal. You will not.

He kicked the door with the toe of his shoe, again and again, until his foot was aching. Then he backed up and kicked it one more time with his heel. It was a good kick, solid and square. So good, that the recoil from that kick sent Carlo tumbling backward down the steps where he fell onto the front walk.

Carlo lay listening to dead air.

My God, it's as quiet as a church out here.

He began to giggle. Whatever this was, it was starting to feel good to him . . . finally good . . . liquor and sedatives . . . so good.

But then came a bell, a thunderous bell. And when it began to ring in one of the towers above Carlo's head, incredibly brash, unquestionably commanding and frightening as hell, it brought Carlo far enough out of his stupor to get him to see that committing suicide might not be what God had been telling him to do.

With each strike of the bell's clapper, Carlo opened his eyes wider and roused himself a little more until he was sitting upright, staring at the full moon between the towers of the church. Twelve times the bell rang and with every ring, the eye of the moon felt like it was getting closer, burning Carlo's third eye, causing him to feel sicker and sicker in his stomach while at the same time somehow *enlightening* him from the inside out.

Leaning over to one side, Carlo braced himself and vomited across the concrete. The bell stopped. Panting, Carlo quivered in place on all fours, smelling the contents of his stomach rising off the sidewalk.

Desperate to get away from the mess he had made, he began crawling out of the moonlight toward a lawn that bordered the church. He'd already landed on that cool carpet of damp grass when a siren broke in, screaming in the distance. It got louder and as it did, Carlo began to understand what God had in mind for him.

He'd done everything he thought God had been telling him to do. He'd gone to a doctor, he'd considered giving back what was left of the money, he went to his wife and children looking for their love, to his brother—his disgusting criminal brother—looking for money. He'd gone so far as to offer his life to God. But none of that was what God had wanted.

The siren was a block away now, so close that the light of the moon was beginning to mingle with the flashing lights of the patrol car.

What God had planned for him was to have him hauled away and humiliated like the failed son of immigrant trash he had turned out to be.

Behind him, the police car—its siren winding down—was shining its headlamps on Carlo. Imprinting his shadow on the door of the church.

"I confess," he said, baying at the moon. "I *am* my father. I *am* my brothers."

He put his hands above his head and turned to face into the lights of the patrol car. He was more than happy to let the light blind him. More than thankful he could not see these men who God had sent to save him with the truth.

THE SON OF THE SHEIK

Vittorio rose from the coffin to join the men standing at the back of the room. Strange to have a body so fluid and light after eighty-four years living in a body as dense as the box in which it now rested. The men at the back of the viewing room were laughing at a joke and it had made Vittorio curious. Arriving at their circle, he watched as the old man who'd been telling the joke threw back his head in laughter. Seizing the opportunity, Vittorio thrust his hand upward into the man's mouth, sliding it though the soft palate, hoping to find the brain behind the joke.

But there was no brain. Not one that Vittorio could put his hand on. He wasn't sure why he was no longer able to grab hold of things, but he wouldn't have been surprised if Joe Martone never had a brain. Comical, how he had to die to find out that Joe's head was empty. Though it wasn't all that funny to realize that he could still see the world but was no longer able to touch it.

Vittorio was removing his hand from Joe's head, when his second son Eddy approached the group. He'd crossed the room from where he'd been sitting perpendicular to the coffin alongside his brothers, their wives and his mother, Aida. Looking at his father but not seeing him—looking *through* him would be a better way to put it—Eddy smirked in that way that had always made Vittorio furious but this morning did nothing to him at all.

How odd it was that he couldn't feel anything when he saw Eddy—anger or love, sadness or disappointment. The same thing happened when he looked at his wife and family sitting by the coffin. Nothing. No feelings at all.

As emotional as he had been all his life, he hadn't been able to feel anything stronger than a distant, shadowy longing, a desire to desire, ever since his heart stopped two days ago. October 9, 1982. The date they'd carve into his headstone.

"Hiya, Joe." Eddy put a hand on Joe's shoulder. "You showing these guys a good time?"

The group laughed again. If he could have, Vittorio would have snapped at his son for the disrespect he was showing in the presence of the dead. It was just like his Charlie-good-time gangster of a son to find a way to keep the laughs coming at his father's funeral. How could his own son, who he had loved so much, act this way?

"You know my boy John?" said Eddy. He raked his hand outward toward a young man who had his chin resting on his sternum and his shoulders pressed against a wall. The group widened to greet him as he raised his chin to meet his father's gaze, whereupon his head fell back into the cavity of his chest.

Twenty-five years old, eyes closing, knuckles punching a jagged outline into the pockets of a pair of suit pants belonging to his father, his grandson John appeared to Vittorio to have been defeated by gravity. Not that gravity meant that much any longer to Vittorio Santorelli.

"Johnny," Eddy shouted. "Say hello to your grandfather's friends."

John raised his head. Mumbling, he pushed himself off the wall and stumbled away from the group, cutting across what appeared to him to be empty space but which was the space occupied by his grandfather. Vittorio shuddered. For a moment, as his grandson had moved within him, Vittorio could feel again. Not his own feelings, but his grandson's. A swirl of disgust edged with melancholy and laced with a note of hatred. For what or for whom Vittorio did not know. Or maybe he didn't want to know, given that the most logical suspect was the boy's father, Eddy, the bad seed that Vittorio had raised: a thief and maybe even a murderer who took great pride in his crimes, and who—he had to face it—was a reflection of Vittorio himself.

Vittorio called out to John. But, as it was with everyone else, the boy did not hear him.

For a time after he died, Vittorio tried to communicate with the living. First in the hospital where he passed, and then in the basement of this funeral parlor where they drained his blood and replaced it with the formaldehyde that would keep him as pickled as a jar of peppers inside his box in the ground for the next hundred years. He had initially tried speaking in English, the adopted language he'd worked at perfecting for years in an attempt to triumph in America. When that failed, he'd tried Italian. Either way, no one could hear him. Not the nurses or doctors. Not the mortician. Not his family. This was a new way around things that he could not get used to after so many years of turning a phrase, punctuating his speech with questions, speaking in quotes he'd stumbled upon from some politician or celebrity he'd read about in *Il Progresso*. Vittorio had thought of his voice as a tool. He could picture himself on the dais of the Saint Anthony fundraisers. Oh how he loved making speeches, trilling his *R*'s, snapping his consonants, his voice a magnet pulling donations from the old women at the tables in the front eating him up like *cavatelli*.

But now his voice, the lightly accented tenor he'd nurtured and prized, no longer registered with others. He would have been angry about it if he could have worked up the passion. But he couldn't, even when John ignored him and walked away.

"Your kid alright?" Joe asked Eddy. "He seems a little . . . confused."

"He's fine," said Eddy defensively.

Drugs. Liquor. Eddy wasn't fooling anybody about his son. Vittorio knew about the boy's problems. An otherwise strong young man like John leaning against a wall to stay upright, was not "fine." How could anyone with eyes in their head think otherwise?

"Anyway," said Joe Martone, changing the subject. "Here's to your old man. He was some kind of guy, that one."

The men laughed.

Why the hell were they laughing at that?

"Yeah," replied Eddy. "He had his faults, God rest his soul."

They men nodded, and then breath by breath, their laughter lapsed into silence.

If he weren't dead, Vittorio would have slapped all of them, starting with Eddy. "Faults?" What did any of them know about faults or overcoming them? Not one of them had tried half has hard to turn himself into a more cultured man. All those nights had he spent bent over his kitchen table working on himself after his family was asleep. There he'd sit, picking his way through books of speeches and soliloquies he'd checked out of the library on Elm Street, squinting at himself in the mirror, eyes sincere, reciting aloud, slowing down to wrap his mind and his mouth around the English words he had not yet mastered. Practicing for a more celebrated American life that would never come. Laboring to smooth off the rough edges. The *faults*.

"*A salute,*" said Joe. "Hopefully he's in a better place."

A better place? I'm right here, you donkey.

Tired, and it was odd that the only thing he *could* still feel was tired, Vittorio let his spirit drift until he found an empty chair in the last row of the viewing room. In this spirit-body where he resided, resting in a chair no longer meant much to him, but he'd spotted two more of his grandsons in the last row and, though neither of them had ever been much of a consolation for him, he had a dim hope that he might find some comfort parking himself for a while there beside them. There was Angie, the son of his third son Angelo and there was Charlie, the son of his oldest, Carlo.

"Stop it, Charlie. We can't." Angie was whining, squirming uncomfortably in his chair.

Vittorio could see that the boy was trying to wriggle out of some scheme his cousin was proposing. Angie had grown from a chubby nervous runt into a timid young man, and when he was alive Vittorio had gone between wanting to protect him and wanting to slap him to get him to act like more than a beaten dog—a creature not unlike his own sad sack of a father, Vittorio's son, Angelo, a pitiful man who lived in his own head, fantasizing he deserved better and blaming everyone but himself when nothing better came his way. His grandson Charlie, on the other hand, was a wisecracking slacker who'd become a thorn in the side of his family; not that his father Carlo didn't deserve it with the way he treated his children as property, no less than the properties he sold to invest in schemes that had more than once put him trouble with the law.

He would have liked to get into it with these boys right here, to set them straight once and for all and help them move past their fathers' troubles and shortcomings. But if he couldn't do it while he was alive, what made him think he'd have any chance to do it now that he was dead?

The thought began to haunt him, and he found himself becoming restless, ping-ponging around the room. It was clear in a way it hadn't been before that—despite how much he had loved them—the men in this family had failed to live up to his hopes for them. He began to wonder if that was the reason his spirit had hung around for the past two days. Was he looking to his sons or grandsons for a sign that he'd done a better job with them and that it was all right for him to exit this world? If so, nothing he'd seen today convinced him that was true.

"Daddy?"

The word caught him by surprise. He'd been snaking above a small knot of people in the back left corner of the room and, when he dropped in closer to investigate the source of the word, he discovered that it had come from a small girl, the half-Black, half-White six-year-old daughter of his youngest grandson, Genie. Her name was Alice, and she'd been hidden among the adults surrounding her as she sat with her legs dangling from the seat of a metal folding chair. Unfurling her hand, she poked at her father who was standing with his back to her.

"Daddy . . ." she said again.

Vittorio leaned closer to get a better look at her coiled black hair bursting above golden-brown features so full and perfect they might have been sculpted by Michelangelo. His great-granddaughter, a beauty he had to admit. So unlike any of the children any of his other offspring had produced. He'd never gotten quite so close to her before. Vittorio's youngest son, Gino, had made it clear that he didn't want much to do with his son, Genie, after the boy had gotten his Black girlfriend pregnant when both of them were in their teens. The two of them all these years later, living together with their child in the basement apartment of a housing project on Congress Avenue. Genie had always let his head follow his heart, while his father, Gino, a crooked police detective about to retire with a full pension, had a heart that had grown into a rock. How his grandson had gotten past his father to slip this child into the funeral home this morning, Vittorio could only guess. Though there was something about having her here that was causing him to remember what it was like to have a heart beating in his own chest.

He brushed his fingers against a strand of the hair that had corkscrewed over the girl's forehead. It did not move. All the same, she flinched.

"Daddy," she called a third time, her voice rising, more uncertain.

"What?" said Genie, stooping beside her.

Ignoring her father, the girl stared directly at Vittorio.

"Son of a bitch," Vittorio whispered. "She knows I'm here."

Seizing the moment, he began to dance like a puppet, trying to get the girl's attention. He could always get a room to laugh when he danced. So why not try to bring some joy into the life of this child? Maybe *that* was the reason he was still half-alive in this room.

He shook his hips, flapping his hands in tandem. He popped his eyes and stuck out his tongue. No one in the room took any notice, of course, except for the girl who continued to watch him, visibly perplexed.

"Here I am," sang Vittorio. "Here I am."

Sliding off her chair, the child took a step closer to him.

"Where you going?" asked her father.

Pausing, she peeked around the spot where Vittorio was dancing to find his lifeless body across the room in the coffin.

Then she started to cry.

At first it was merely a little girl whimpering at the back of a funeral parlor. Within seconds, however, it rose to a full-throated sob. After that it became a wail that turned every head in the viewing room.

As soon as she heard it, Vittorio's wife, Aida, was up and scampering toward Alice from her beachhead of chairs beside the coffin. Crouching down in front of the girl, Aida pushed aside her grandson Genie who didn't seem to have a clue as to how to handle the situation.

Watching it all, Vittorio had stopped dancing.

"Be quiet," said Aida to the child. "Why you crying?"

"I'm scared," said Alice. "I'm sad."

"Stop. You can't cry like that in here. If you gonna cry, we gotta take you outside."

The girl hiccupped, yelping loudly on her exhale. Aida turned to her grandson. "You gotta take her outside."

At that moment, even lacking emotions, he could not fathom how he might have ever let himself get married to such a woman. Alice was a child—a little girl who'd been rejected. Trying to comfort her had comforted *him*. Plus she was crying over him, her great grandfather. Would Aida have to die before she understood how wrongheaded she was acting?

Hug her, woman, he thought. *She knows I'm here, even if you don't. Even if nobody else does, the girl knows I'm around. She needs you.*

"Come on." Aida wrangled the girl by her shoulder, slotting her roughly into her father's arms until he began to escort her away. "Take her outside."

There was nothing to be done. No action he could take to get his wife or any of his kin to understand how this little girl, no matter the color of her skin, had a rightful place in his family.

Maybe *that* was the reason his sons had turned out as they had. He knew what it was like to be treated as less than human when you looked or spoke differently from the people around you. Maybe his sons had been cursed simply by being born in an America that had done that to him and in ways he could only imagine to them as well.

As a boy in Italy, an ocean away, he'd pictured America as a golden city that stretched from sea to sea. He nurtured his dreams, learned to read, and took pride in how he dressed, fantasizing an American life with a soundtrack of syncopated music and a backdrop of tall buildings where electric lights burned day and night. As he got older he even romanticized that he would escape here to marry an "American girl" and find his fortune with her on his arm.

But he'd been saddled in an arranged marriage with Aida; plain, uninspired, sullen Aida. When he finally did get to America and immediately started having children—four boys who lived, another girl who did not—he swallowed his pride and tried to make his dreams come true by taking any job that halfway fit his view of himself as an important man. The problem was that in this country each group of immigrants that arrived had a nasty habit of handing down the bigotry they faced to the next group that got here. So that, time and again, he found he was belittled and overlooked by the Irishmen and Jews who were his bosses at those very jobs that he didn't want in the first place.

Jobs where he was ridiculed and insulted because of the way he spoke or the way he moved his hands when he spoke or—most infuriating of all—because other men were threatened by his looks and charisma.

Goddamn it. In this country he could have been a movie star. Another Valentino. If only he'd been given the chance. He was handsome and seductive like his idol in *The Son of the Sheik*. He spoke more eloquently than any of the transplanted Italians around him. He could have been famous: an immigrant rising. If only he could have been who he truly was.

If he had, maybe his boys would have gotten somewhere too. Maybe his sons and then the sons of his sons would have realized the dreams that this country had promised them. But as it was—and watching them this morning he had no reason to think otherwise— his boys had followed in his hobbled footsteps. Each of his sons had failed in their own way and each had passed that failure down to *their* sons like a virus. Whether they'd gotten a job as a cop or as a criminal, whether they bought and sold property to make themselves rich or they'd stumbled from one low-paying job to the next. All of his sons and grandsons, too, were broken men—resentful and small-minded, downhearted, lost or fearful. And though they would never admit it to themselves, Vittorio had to face the fact that his boys had been broken because of how this country had broken *him*, little by little, until he became the unhappy, angry man who was their father.

"You okay, Mom? You need anything?"

Eddy had stepped away from his father's friends to find his mother.

"I don't want nothing," said Aida, turning her back on her son and her husband's ancient confederates, choosing to walk back to the coffin in rage.

Paddling through the air, Vittorio swam toward his wife.

"Aida. Wait. Please."

He wanted to tell her what he'd realized. To swallow his pride and admit that so much of what had happened to them had been his doing. Reaching her, he put his arms around her body, but his hands only doubled back around himself.

Vittorio cupped Aida's face with his hands. He could recall the panicked expression on that face the first time he touched her on their wedding night more than half a century ago.

She had not wanted to be married to him as he had not wanted to be married to her. It was a fact he could no longer bury under his own bitterness. Forced to reckon with himself, he thought of how he had abused and insulted her. How she had worked day and night to keep order in their crowded railroad flat, trying to feed his ungrateful children on the money he brought home, and how he had cursed her for not being able to do more with the pittance she'd been given. He recalled how he ignored her and let her sleep alone, how he had caused her to grow old before her time while he ran around with other woman.

God forgive him.

"Good morning, everyone." The funeral director had made his way to the front to address the mourners. "If I could have your attention." He took out a prayer card. "Before we go to the cemetery, I'd like to ask you to join us in a prayer for Vittorio." He made the sign of the cross.

"Our Father . . . in heaven . . ."

Vittorio was only able to make out a word or two in every eight or ten of the words being recited.

" . . . Thy Name . . . Be Done . . . Hour . . . This day . . . Bread . . ."

The harder he tried to tune into the prayer, the more intermittent the words became until after a moment, they stopped altogether. He could see lips moving but there was no sound.

Wriggling around inside the silence, Vittorio began to struggle, until, against his will, he started to rise. Reaching the ceiling, he continued on through the plaster and beams, coming out the other side into the open air. Before he realized what was going on, he had pierced the canopy of trees surrounding the building and come to a halt, suspended between the clouds and the earth.

This was not the way he had expected it to end.

Below him were the vehicles waiting to escort his body to the graveyard: the limousines parked bumper-to-bumper; the sedans and station wagons belonging to those who'd come to grieve; the white hearse at the mouth of the driveway. He could see the men and woman who'd left the viewing room to huddle under the portico in front of the funeral home.

Here too, not unlike the words of the prayer, everything below was fading as he struggled to take it in. His life was becoming a color photograph that had been hung for too many years in the sunlight—reds becoming pinks, blues melting into grays, greens and yellows almost interchangeable, flesh tones and facial features bleached almost white.

Looked at the other way around, the earth wasn't fading from him as much as he was fading from the earth. As hard as it would have been to admit it moments ago, his disappearing was turning out to be more pleasurable than he had ever imagined it would be. For two days he'd been resisting it, and now that he was actually leaving, it was not that bad at all. Dying was easier than living had ever been.

What a thing to realize at the end. That his life had only been a test to see how much he could endure, a test he could never pass but could never truly fail either.

Far below, the doors to the funeral home sprung open and his coffin emerged. By then, he could not make out the features of the men holding its handles, but from the stoop of their shoulders and the heavy plant of their feet, he knew that these were his sons and grandsons carrying his body. In this same way, he calculated that the women dressed in black flocking behind the coffin were his sons' wives, and in their wake, a foot or two behind, another woman who he judged to be Aida. She was dragging a small child along behind her —their great granddaughter, Alice.

He couldn't have told you how he knew, but in that moment he understood that they would all be fine without him. They would survive him and whatever he had or hadn't done for them. Over time, they might even forgive him. At the very least, they would never forget him.

He would go on living until every last one of them was gone.

On the ground below, Alice broke free of her great grandmother's hand. Tilting her head to the sky, she lifted her hand to shade her eyes from the sun, fluttering her fingers. It was a gesture that the people who saw her would later on describe, somewhat sentimentally, as a little girl waving at the sky.

Okay, said Vittorio. *Lasciami andare*. I'm ready.

In saying these words, Vittorio did not know to whom he was speaking. Moreover, a fraction of a second after saying them, he did not know he had ever said them. Having accepted that he had done all he could with this version of his life, Vittorio had truly vanished. His seeing unplugged. His hearing switched off. All memories erased and emotions shredded. All black. Nothing left of Vittorio Santorelli but the empty body in which he had lived.

Except that somewhere, outside of time as Vittorio would have known it, music was playing in a movie palace. Cymbals and tambours and the winding wail of flutes. Sultry strings beckoned, and a chorus of voices cried out, coaxing desert sands onto the screen. A title card appeared superimposed over the desert: *Rudolf Valentino in "The Son of the Sheik."*

In the audience of this theater was a row of kids, agog, their faces lit with movie light. Their mouths watering in anticipation of the silent life unspooling before them. Valentino made his entrance and before turning his attention to the dancing girl who would become his movie wife, he lowered his eyes, nearly imperceptibly, to glance at the youngsters in the second row.

If only those children knew his real name and from whom he had transcended. He'd always thought that children could see him in a way no one else could. If only they could know how far back in time he'd had to travel to get here. If only he himself could remember the name Vittorio Santorelli in those moments off the screen when he was more than a flicker of light.

It was a pity how all that had to be left behind.

ABOUT THE AUTHOR

TONY TADDEI was born and raised in New Haven, Connecticut. His humor and fiction have appeared in publications including *Story Magazine*, *Folio*, *New Millennium Writings*, *The Funny Times*, *Pif Magazine*, *Animal*, and *The Florida Review*. Tony holds an MFA from the prestigious Bennington College Writing Seminars Program and is a recipient of the New Jersey State Council on the Arts Fellowship for fiction. A trained actor, for many years Tony created characters on stage before turning his attention to inventing life on the page. Tony currently resides in New Jersey, where he raised three daughters and lives with his wife, Karen, and their two-year-old cockapoo, Brodie.

ROBERT ZWEIG. *Return to Naples*. Vol 70. Memoir.

AIROS & CAPPELLI. *Guido*. Vol 69. Italian/American Studies.

FRED GARDAPHÉ. *Moustache Pete is Dead! Long Live Moustache Pete!*.
   Vol 67. Literature/Oral History.

PAOLO RUFFILLI. *Dark Room/Camera oscura*. Vol 66. Poetry.

HELEN BAROLINI. *Crossing the Alps*. Vol 65. Fiction.

COSMO FERRARA. *Profiles of Italian Americans*. Vol 64. Italian Americana.

GIL FAGIANI. *Chianti in Connecticut*. Vol 63. Poetry.

BASSETTI & D'ACQUINO. *Italic Lessons*. Vol 62. Italian/American Studies.

CAVALIERI & PASCARELLI, Eds. *The Poet's Cookbook*. Vol 61. Poetry/Recipes.

EMANUEL DI PASQUALE. *Siciliana*. Vol 60. Poetry.

NATALIA COSTA, Ed. *Bufalini*. Vol 59. Poetry.

RICHARD VETERE. *Baroque*. Vol 58. Fiction.

LEWIS TURCO. *La Famiglia/The Family*. Vol 57. Memoir.

NICK JAMES MILETI. *The Unscrupulous*. Vol 56. Humanities.

BASSETTI. ACCOLLA. D'AQUINO. *Italici: An Encounter with Piero Bassetti*.
   Vol 55. Italian Studies.

GIOSE RIMANELLI. *The Three-legged One*. Vol 54. Fiction.

CHARLES KLOPP. *Bele Antiche Stòrie*. Vol 53. Criticism.

JOSEPH RICAPITO. *Second Wave*. Vol 52. Poetry.

GARY MORMINO. *Italians in Florida*. Vol 51. History.

GIANFRANCO ANGELUCCI. *Federico F.* Vol 50. Fiction.

ANTHONY VALERIO. *The Little Sailor*. Vol 49. Memoir.

ROSS TALARICO. *The Reptilian Interludes*. Vol 48. Poetry.

RACHEL GUIDO DE VRIES. *Teeny Tiny Tino's Fishing Story*.
   Vol 47. Children's Literature.

EMANUEL DI PASQUALE. *Writing Anew*. Vol 46. Poetry.

MARIA FAMÀ. *Looking For Cover*. Vol 45. Poetry.

ANTHONY VALERIO. *Toni Cade Bambara's One Sicilian Night*. Vol 44. Poetry.

EMANUEL CARNEVALI. *Furnished Rooms*. Vol 43. Poetry.

BRENT ADKINS. et al., Ed. *Shifting Borders. Negotiating Places*.
   Vol 42. Conference.

GEORGE GUIDA. *Low Italian*. Vol 41. Poetry.

GARDAPHÈ, GIORDANO, TAMBURRI. *Introducing Italian Americana*.
   Vol 40. Italian/American Studies.

DANIELA GIOSEFFI. *Blood Autumn/Autunno di sangue*. Vol 39. Poetry.

FRED MISURELLA. *Lies to Live By*. Vol 38. Stories.

STEVEN BELLUSCIO. *Constructing a Bibliography*. Vol 37. Italian Americana.

ANTHONY JULIAN TAMBURRI, Ed. *Italian Cultural Studies 2002*.
   Vol 36. Essays.

BEA TUSIANI. *con amore*. Vol 35. Memoir.

FLAVIA BRIZIO-SKOV, Ed. *Reconstructing Societies in the Aftermath of War*.
   Vol 34. History.

TAMBURRI. et al., Eds. *Italian Cultural Studies 2001*. Vol 33. Essays.

ELIZABETH G. MESSINA, Ed. *In Our Own Voices*.
   Vol 32. Italian/American Studies.

STANISLAO G. PUGLIESE. *Desperate Inscriptions.* Vol 31. History.
HOSTERT & TAMBURRI, Eds. *Screening Ethnicity.*
  Vol 30. Italian/American Culture.
G. PARATI & B. LAWTON, Eds. *Italian Cultural Studies.* Vol 29. Essays.
HELEN BAROLINI. *More Italian Hours.* Vol 28. Fiction.
FRANCO NASI, Ed. *Intorno alla Via Emilia.* Vol 27. Culture.
ARTHUR L. CLEMENTS. *The Book of Madness & Love.* Vol 26. Poetry.
JOHN CASEY, et al. *Imagining Humanity.* Vol 25. Interdisciplinary Studies.
ROBERT LIMA. *Sardinia/Sardegna.* Vol 24. Poetry.
DANIELA GIOSEFFI. *Going On.* Vol 23. Poetry.
ROSS TALARICO. *The Journey Home.* Vol 22. Poetry.
EMANUEL DI PASQUALE. *The Silver Lake Love Poems.* Vol 21. Poetry.
JOSEPH TUSIANI. *Ethnicity.* Vol 20. Poetry.
JENNIFER LAGIER. *Second Class Citizen.* Vol 19. Poetry.
FELIX STEFANILE. *The Country of Absence.* Vol 18. Poetry.
PHILIP CANNISTRARO. *Blackshirts.* Vol 17. History.
LUIGI RUSTICHELLI, Ed. *Seminario sul racconto.* Vol 16. Narrative.
LEWIS TURCO. *Shaking the Family Tree.* Vol 15. Memoirs.
LUIGI RUSTICHELLI, Ed. *Seminario sulla drammaturgia.*
  Vol 14. Theater/Essays.
FRED GARDAPHÈ. *Moustache Pete is Dead! Long Live Moustache Pete!.*
  Vol 13. Oral Literature.
JONE GAILLARD CORSI. *Il libretto d'autore. 1860 - 1930.* Vol 12. Criticism.
HELEN BAROLINI. *Chiaroscuro: Essays of Identity.* Vol 11. Essays.
PICARAZZI & FEINSTEIN, Eds. *An African Harlequin in Milan.*
  Vol 10. Theater/Essays.
JOSEPH RICAPITO. *Florentine Streets & Other Poems.* Vol 9. Poetry.
FRED MISURELLA. *Short Time.* Vol 8. Novella.
NED CONDINI. *Quartettsatz.* Vol 7. Poetry.
ANTHONY JULIAN TAMBURRI, Ed. *Fuori: Essays by Italian/American
  Lesbiansand Gays.* Vol 6. Essays.
ANTONIO GRAMSCI. P. Verdicchio. Trans. & Intro. *The Southern Question.*
  Vol 5. Social Criticism.
DANIELA GIOSEFFI. *Word Wounds & Water Flowers.* Vol 4. Poetry. $8
WILEY FEINSTEIN. *Humility's Deceit: Calvino Reading Ariosto Reading Calvino.*
  Vol 3. Criticism.
PAOLO A. GIORDANO, Ed. *Joseph Tusiani: Poet. Translator. Humanist.*
  Vol 2. Criticism.
ROBERT VISCUSI. *Oration Upon the Most Recent Death of Christopher Columbus.*
  Vol 1. Poetry.

www.ingramcontent.com/pod-product-compliance
Lightning Source LLC
Chambersburg PA
CBHW020021030726
47499CB00007B/2221